Molly and the Cat Café

MELISSA DALEY

Molly and the Cat Café

MACMILLAN

First published 2015 by Macmillan
an imprint of Pan Macmillan
20 New Wharf Road, London N1 9RR
Associated companies throughout the world
www.panmacmillan.com

ISBN 978-1-5098-0429-0

1 3 5 7 9 8 6 4 2

A CIP catalogue record for this book is available from the British Library.

Cat illustrations by Ray and Corinne Burrows (Beehive Illustration)

Printed and bound by CPI Group (UK) Ltd, Croydon, CR0 4YY

Visit **www.panmacmillan.com** to read more about all our books
and to buy them. You will also find features, author interviews and
news of any author events, and you can sign up for e-newsletters
so that you're always first to hear about our new releases.

For Suse and Louis

Behind every successful woman
there is often a rather talented cat
Anon

Molly and the Cat Café

1

I don't remember much from my early kittenhood, but when I close my eyes I can vividly recall the delight on Margery's face when I was placed on her lap for the first time, a mewling ball of tabby fluff.

'Well now, who's this?' she said gently, as I gazed up at her with not-long-opened eyes.

Margery's friend answered, 'This little thing is Molly. She's eight weeks old. Her mother was a stray. The others from the litter have all been homed, so she's the last to go.'

I squinted into Margery's face as I sat on her lap. Her skin was soft and downy, settling into deep folds around her kind-looking eyes. She had short silver hair carefully groomed into waves that framed her face. But what I remember most about Margery in those days is her smile. It was a smile that made me feel I was the most important thing in her world or, as Margery would have put it, 'the best thing since sliced bread'.

'I thought you could do with some companionship,' the friend continued. 'I know you've been lonely, since Malcolm passed away. A nice lap-cat could be just what the doctor ordered.'

'Well, I think Molly is . . . the cat's whiskers.' Margery answered softly, and there was no mistaking the pleasure in her voice.

And, with that, it was settled: Margery was to be my owner. She tickled me under the chin and I started to purr, tentatively at first, but as I relaxed my purr grew to a loud, steady rumble. Margery began to laugh at how much noise 'a little scrap' like me could produce.

As the months passed and I grew from kitten to young adult cat, Margery and I established a cosy partnership, based on mutual adoration. Margery enjoyed having someone to talk to and take care of, and I relished being the object of her loving attention. As an active, growing youngster, I was constantly hungry, and Margery seemed to delight in my insatiable appetite. She not only bought me the choicest cat food available, but would also make sure to save a portion of her own meals for me: chicken, lamb chops, a nice piece of salmon – whatever Margery cooked, there was always a Molly-sized portion put to one side in a dish on the counter.

Margery's house quickly became my domain: I could nap where I chose and do whatever I liked. With such a comfortable life indoors, I never particularly felt the need to explore the world outside Margery's home. From her bedroom window I could see the roofs of houses in the village and the rolling slopes of the fields that lay beyond. I did, on occasion, wander out of our cul-de-sac, but to be honest the village we lived in held no great appeal for me. There was not much to it: a parade of shops, a church and a couple of pubs. I knew that other cats from the village enjoyed hunting in the churchyard; but, being so well fed at home, I rarely put my hunting skills into practice.

You are probably thinking I was lucky, and I would have to agree with you. Life with Margery was all that a cat could hope for, and I loved everything about it. But that was before Margery's sadness started.

'There you go, Molly,' Margery whispered one day, when I was about a year old. She bent over, using one hand to steady herself on the kitchen worktop, and placed my food bowl carefully on the linoleum floor. I began to purr in anticipation, I was hungry, and had been waiting patiently while Margery moved slowly around the kitchen, completing the domestic chores that always preceded my teatime.

I hopped down from the kitchen table, but a quick look in my bowl confirmed my worst fears. I sniffed warily at the contents, hoping that the beige-coloured mushy substance might conceal something feline-friendly, but my hope quickly turned to disappointment.

'It's mashed potato, Molly – your favourite,' Margery said helpfully, noticing my reluctance. Suspecting this was the only meal I was going to be offered, I gingerly licked the contents of the bowl. With trepidation I took a tiny mouthful. The taste was bland and the consistency lumpy, and as I attempted to swallow it, I realized something solid had become lodged in the back of my throat. I felt my body spasm as I retched the offending mouthful back up onto the linoleum. I peered at it closely. It was a piece of unmashed potato, grey-looking and inedible. Not for the first time in recent weeks I realized that an evening hunting expedition would be required to satisfy my appetite.

Trying to ignore the hunger pangs in my stomach, I glanced up at Margery, who was now busying herself at the kitchen sink. Something about the way she was muttering worried me. I had grown familiar with her domestic routines (she had carried out the same tasks every day for as long as I could remember), but I could sense that she was feeling uncertain and anxious. She carefully washed up a saucepan in the sink, taking time to dry it thoroughly with a tea towel. Afterwards she stood clutching the pan to her chest, looking nervously around the kitchen. She opened the fridge and placed the pan inside, then tutted to herself and removed it again. She proceeded to open the doors of various kitchen cupboards, frustrated to find them full of glasses or chinaware. I knew this was not her normal behaviour; or, rather, it hadn't been normal in the past, but there was no escaping the fact that incidents like these had been happening increasingly frequently of late.

Leaving my bowl of sludgy mashed potato behind, I padded across the kitchen and stood in front of the one cupboard that she had not yet checked. Standing proudly with my tail erect, I meowed loudly.

Margery was looking around the kitchen distractedly, and it took a few yowls to attract her attention.

'What is it, Molly?' she asked, her tone slightly irritated.

I rubbed my head profusely against the cupboard door, willing her to understand my gesture.

Margery paused and stared at me vacantly for a moment, before leaning down and pulling the cupboard door open. 'Oh, Molly, you clever girl!' she exclaimed, on seeing a neat stack of saucepans inside. She placed the pan in its rightful place, then rubbed me behind the ears. I purred, touched by her gratitude, but underneath I felt a sense of disquiet deep within me.

Margery and I had been through this routine countless times in recent months. I had grown adept at watching her movements closely, noting whenever she did anything out of the ordinary, such as placing her reading glasses in the fridge or her house keys in the bathroom cabinet. When, as inevitably happened after such an occurrence, she became distressed, I would help her retrace her steps, meowing at the spot where I knew the missing item to be. At first I thought it was a game that she and I were playing together, and I congratulated myself on my powers of observation and memory. But over time I noticed that Margery didn't enjoy the game as much as I did. In fact she was often upset and agitated, scolding herself for her stupidity.

From the outside, our life looked as though nothing had changed: Margery still pottered around the house, dusting and tidying while I dozed on the sofa, and I did my best to help her with the crossword, by sitting on the newspaper and batting at her pen while she filled in the empty squares. But she was smiling less and less, and sometimes I would find her crying in the armchair as she gazed out of the window. I did my best to comfort her, rubbing up against her cheek and purring loudly, but I sensed something was wrong that was beyond my power to fix.

There were the lapses in memory, the befuddlement, the anxiety about lost chequebooks and misplaced keys. These were infrequent at first, but gradually they became more common, until eventually they became the norm. Even with my observation skills to help guide her, Margery seemed to be losing her grip on the day-to-day practicalities of her life. Of *our* life.

Having placed the clean saucepan in its correct cupboard that day, Margery went into the living room to watch television. I considered curling up alongside her to spend the evening in companionable silence, but I was hungry and I knew from experience that I could not count on Margery to remember to feed me again that evening. I had a cursory sniff of the cold mashed potato, which had begun to congeal in my bowl, before slipping out through the cat flap, on the hunt for some small rodent to supplement my dinner.

When I returned home later that evening, Margery had gone to bed. I performed my usual night-time patrol around the house, checking that all the windows were closed, the front door was locked and the oven had not been left on. Satisfied that the house was safe and secure, I curled up on the sofa and went to sleep.

The following morning I was having a wash on the living-room windowsill, listening to the sounds upstairs as Margery moved slowly around her bedroom, getting dressed and brushing her hair. I hoped today would be a good day for Margery and me: that she wouldn't be tearful, and that she would remember to give me breakfast. Hearing her tentative steps on the stairs, I jumped down from the windowsill.

Watching her closely, to make sure she negotiated safely the twist at the bottom of the stairs, I trotted out of the living room with my tail up in greeting. I chirruped a 'hello' and rubbed up against her ankles.

'Oh!' she exclaimed.

I purred in reply.

'Who are you?' she asked. I looked up at Margery and saw that familiar confusion in her eyes, beneath a furrowed brow.

I meowed at her. 'I'm Molly,' I wanted to say. 'I'm your cat!'

She tilted her head to one side, looking at me quizzically. I willed her to recognize me, to say my name again and laughingly reassure me that she could never forget who I was.

'Have you come from down the street, puss? You need to be getting home – your owner will be wondering where you've got to.'

She walked past me to the front door and picked up the keys, which just the previous evening I had checked were in their correct place on the shelf. She carefully unlocked the door, struggling with the chain for a couple of moments before pulling it open. Then she smiled at me, evidently expecting me to be grateful that I was being released, free to go home. I stood on the hall carpet, my tail twitching.

'Well, go on then. I expect you'll be wanting your breakfast soon.'

I could feel my eyes start to prickle. Margery's disorientation had often left me bewildered, and her distress at those moments when she seemed to comprehend what was happening to her had made my heart ache. But never before had I felt pain like this. This was different. It was the pain of not being recognized; of looking into my owner's eyes and seeing not love, but confusion. It was the pain of feeling like a stranger in my own home.

Not wanting Margery to see my suffering, I lowered my head and slipped past her and out through the front door.

2

Margery continued to have good days and bad days, but the bad days far outnumbered the good. I learnt not to feel so hurt when she couldn't remember my name, or appeared to forget my existence until I yowled out of hunger or sheer desperation to be noticed. It felt to me as though Margery was somehow disappearing, vanishing further and further down a tunnel inside her mind. Physically she looked smaller and frailer too, and my fur would prickle with anxiety as I watched her shakily climb the stairs at night.

Margery's son had begun to visit the house more often. He was a small, wiry man who gave off an air of perpetual impatience, as if there was always somewhere else he needed to be. I found him difficult to warm to. I could never get the measure of him, and as much as Margery loved to see him, I sensed that his hurried air made her agitation worse. I wished I could get him to settle and relax, to spend some quality time with his mother, rather than wanting to be on his way as quickly as possible. I tried to encourage him to stay by jumping on his lap whenever he sat down, but he merely shoved me off irritably. I would retreat to another part of the room and try to convey my disapproval from a distance.

'So how are things, Mum? You been looking after yourself?'

'Oh, yes, yes, I'm very well, thank you, David. And how's . . . ?'

I could see Margery's mortification as she struggled to remember her daughter-in-law's name.

'Pat's fine, thanks. The kids are all right too – that is, I think they are. Hardly ever see them these days, to be honest.'

I could see that Margery was thrown, desperately trying to picture who 'the kids' – her grandchildren – were. But David didn't seem to pick up on these cues, and would carry on talking about his family or job as if Margery was fully cognizant of every detail of his life. Margery just smiled politely and tried to follow what he was saying.

She was always upset to say goodbye to David at the end of his visits, and I knew to expect tears after he had gone. Margery couldn't put into words how she was feeling, even to me, but I did what I could to comfort her just through my presence. Usually stroking me seemed to calm her down eventually.

One afternoon in late summer, after an exuberant session of butterfly-chasing in our garden, I crept inside the house and climbed upstairs to find David going through piles of boxes in Margery's spare room. Unable to restrain my innate curiosity (not to mention my feline love of cardboard boxes), I jumped into the midst of the operation to investigate. David had his head inside a large open box, so I found myself nose-to-nose with him amidst a pile of dusty paperwork. Evidently I took him by surprise, because he swore loudly and immediately scooped me out of the box and dropped me onto the floor. Undeterred, I found a stack of cardboard on the other side of the room and spent a pleasant hour exploring whilst keeping an eye on what David was doing.

After a while I settled down inside a box, enjoying the rays of sunshine that were warming it through the window. David seemed to have forgotten I was there.

'For God's sake, Mum, why on earth have you kept all this stuff?' he muttered, and I could hear him roughly shoving piles of paper into a dustbin liner. At one point his mobile phone rang and he swore under his breath, before retrieving it from his back pocket.

'Hiya, Pat, I'm up to my neck in it here. There's

eighty years' worth of rubbish lying on the floor in front of me, and I'm only on the first room.'

David stood up and closed the spare-room door, evidently trying to keep Margery from overhearing the conversation. I watched and listened in silence from my vantage point inside the cardboard box.

'No, I haven't spoken to her about it yet. I know, *I know.*' I could tell he was getting annoyed. 'I've got to time it right. Got to pick the right moment or she'll go to pieces. But I'm making a start by clearing some of this rubbish out. I will tell her – yes, I know, *soon.* But you know what she's like, so determined to be independent.'

Inside my cardboard hiding place I could feel alarm starting to spread around my body. I couldn't imagine what it was that David hadn't told Margery, but it was obviously something that would upset her. I remained still, praying he would say more to enlighten me, but instead he became impatient with Pat and ended the phone call with a curt, 'Look, I've got to get on with this. We'll talk about it later.'

Over the next few weeks David continued to visit the house regularly. He would let himself in and call out to Margery from the hallway, 'Hi, Mum, it's David. I'm here to help you tidy up.'

But what he called 'tidying', I saw as the dismantling of our home, one room at a time. Over and over again he filled the boot of his car with soft furnishings, bags of old clothes and piles of papers, reassuring Margery that it wasn't anything she needed and saying that it was only fit for the tip.

Margery seemed too frightened to protest. Usually she would take herself into another room rather than watch her possessions being ransacked. Occasionally I saw a wistful look in her eye as she studied a pile of belongings that had been earmarked for the charity shop.

I, however, was furious. How dare he come into our home and make completely arbitrary decisions about what Margery – and, for that matter, what *I* – was or wasn't allowed to keep? Time and again I would find that one of my favourite things – a moth-eaten old picnic rug or a hessian foot stool – had been taken to the tip without my knowledge.

The house no longer smelt like home, either. The distinctive scent of lavender, which had always suffused Margery's clothes and furniture, was now smothered by the chemical reek of polish and detergent, so overpowering that they made my eyes water and my throat sore.

During this time I spent my days patrolling the house, attempting to reclaim my territory by rubbing my scent glands on as many surfaces as possible. But it was a hopeless task, in the face of David and his relentless packing, boxing and cleaning. If Margery wasn't around, David made no attempt to hide his dislike of me, shooing me out of the house at every opportunity, although I noticed that in front of Margery he still maintained the pretence of finding me endearing.

There is no doubt in my mind that the upheaval at home made Margery's confusion worse. I could see her deteriorate in front of my eyes. She had all but stopped eating, having given up cooking weeks ago when she could no longer hold all the stages of the process in her mind. She found it difficult to settle – like a wary cat expecting to be attacked – and would repeatedly go to the front window and peer out, as if waiting for something or someone.

I did what I could to try and calm her nerves, but as her distress increased, so did my sense of foreboding. I still didn't know what David planned, but deep down I knew that life for Margery and me was going to change. All I could do was stay close and try and comfort her, whilst taking what reassurance I could from the familiar feel of her hands on my fur, and the smell of her skin.

One afternoon I came into the living room to find Margery in tears, as David sat beside her on the sofa with his arm awkwardly round her shoulder.

'Come on, Mum, you know it's for the best,' he was

saying in a pleading voice. 'It's just not safe for you to be here any more. The stairs are too much for you now, and you know you've been getting forgetful recently.'

Margery said nothing, but wept silently into her cotton handkerchief.

'The Elms is a great place. They'll be able to take proper care of you there. Cook your meals, do your washing and all that. Come on now, it's for the best.' And he embraced her in a clumsy bear hug.

I tiptoed silently out of the living room. My head was spinning and I needed to get some fresh air. I pushed my way through the cat flap and went to sit on the front path. I began to wash, an activity that helps me to order my thoughts as much as my appearance.

At least now I knew the worst, and there was finally an explanation for what had been going on. Margery was going to move out, to live in a place called The Elms. Pausing mid-wash, I looked up and noticed for the first time a wooden 'For Sale' sign attached to the gate at the end of the path. I felt my blood run cold.

My heart ached for Margery, knowing how much she would miss our lovely home, but I also feared for myself. When Margery moved into The Elms and our house was sold, what would become of me?

I slipped back inside through the cat flap and paused outside the living-room door. I could hear Margery's soft sobbing from within, and David's voice was a low, wheedling monotone. I didn't know what was in store for me, but I knew there was one thing that might make me feel better.

I crept past the living-room door to the staircase, where David had placed his shoes neatly next to the bottom step. After a quick glance over my shoulder, I squatted over David's shoes and peed in them. And, fastidious though I am about personal hygiene, it felt good.

3

One morning not long after the shoe incident I was enjoying a quiet meditation in my usual lookout position by the front-room window. Autumn was in the air outside. Leaves were falling onto the street's front lawns and the sky was a leaden grey.

There was not normally much passing traffic in the cul-de-sac, so naturally I noticed when a large lorry turned into the street. As it approached I saw the logo on its side – 'Expert Removals' – and I felt my whiskers vibrate from the rumble of its engine. It drew up slowly in front of Margery's house, then began to reverse into her driveway. Three men jumped out of the cab and started to open up the doors at the rear of the lorry, pulling at straps and sliding heavy bolts, before pressing a button that lowered a platform onto the drive.

I had never seen a removal lorry before, but knew that the uncertainty regarding what was happening to us was about to come to an end. I turned back to look at my surroundings. The sofa where I had spent the night was pushed up against the living-room wall, stripped of its cushions, tartan blanket and lacy armrest covers. The sideboard, armchair and other large items had been placed together in the middle of the floor, with wooden packing crates filling every available space.

I heard the familiar sounds of Margery moving around her bedroom upstairs. I could picture her carefully combing the waves of her hair into position and powdering her nose, before spraying lavender water behind her ears. In spite of the many things about everyday life that she struggled to remember, her morning grooming routine seemed to have survived intact. Although it pained me to think this might be the last time she ever did it in her own home, I also drew some comfort from it: it reassured me that not everything from our life together had been lost.

Soon I heard David's voice outside the front door and the sound of his key in the lock. He was barking instructions to the removal men as he came in, sounding even more impatient and harassed than usual. Instantly the contemplative mood of the front room was shattered, as the men flung open the door and began to manoeuvre the larger items out of the house and into the lorry.

At first I stayed in my spot on the windowsill. I felt

a responsibility to Margery to keep an eye on proceedings and make sure her possessions were treated with due care. But watching my favourite pieces of furniture disappear into the cavernous lorry brought a lump to my throat, and before long I could watch no longer. I arched my back in a stretch, before flexing out to my full length along the windowsill. Then I jumped down and made my way through the living room, being careful to avoid the booted feet all around me.

I considered going outside to get away from the dismantling of my life that was going on inside the house, but it had started to rain, and somehow it felt disloyal to Margery to leave her to face this alone.

Passing the cat carrier sitting ominously in the hallway, I made my way upstairs and found Margery sitting on her bed. She was wearing her blue woollen jacket and a felt hat with a crocheted flower on the rim. It was an outfit that I knew she saved 'for best', and I thought she looked beautiful in it. But when I padded around to her side of the bed, I could see that tears were silently falling into her lap. She made no attempt to stop them, but just sat gazing out of the window.

I chirruped at her, trying to sound cheerful. She looked surprised at first, then looked down at me and smiled. 'Oh, hello, you.'

I wasn't sure whether or not she remembered my name, but at that moment it was enough that she recognized me. I hopped up onto the bed and nestled beside her. Her hand automatically came to stroke me, tickling me behind the ears and under the chin in my favourite way. I purred my loudest purr, doing my best to drown out the noise of the removal men's voices and the lifting and lowering of the lorry's platform.

We remained upstairs on the bed for what felt like a lifetime, while all around us we could hear the men stomping through the house, being chided intermittently by David. Part of me wanted to stay like this forever, but another part just wanted it to be over, for the axe to fall and put us both out of our misery. I will never know whether Margery suspected this would be our last cuddle together, but I felt certain of it. She continued to stroke me and I continued to purr; perhaps we were both trying to reassure ourselves that we would be okay.

'Mum, where are you?'

David's abrasive voice made us jump. He pushed open the bedroom door roughly and I felt the hackles on my back rise. The sight of his mother and me together made him pause for a moment, before he walked round the side of the bed towards us.

'Mum, come on now, it's time to go,' he said. I could tell he was making an effort to sound less impatient, but his insincerity didn't fool me. I was still curled up beside Margery and instinctively began to emit a growl deep in my throat as he approached.

Margery looked at him blankly, and I wondered whether she even remembered who he was or why he was there. For a fleeting moment I envied her, and wondered whether losing my home would hurt less if I did not understand what was happening. Perhaps that would be preferable to the pain I was feeling.

'Yes, yes, of course,' Margery whispered, looking around for her handbag and her scarf. She stood up slowly, and David took her elbow in a show of concern, which I knew belied his desire to hurry her up. I was still growling, in an involuntary expression of distrust.

'That's enough from you, cat,' David said, batting me off the bare mattress as he guided Margery round the corner of the bed. I sat angrily on the landing, listening as he led Margery down the stairs and out through the front door. A few minutes later the car doors slammed and I heard him drive away. The removal men bustled past me into Margery's bedroom and began to take apart her bed.

'Are we meant to be taking the cat or what?' one of them asked.

'Nah, David's coming back for it later, so he said,' the other replied.

I sometimes wonder how my life might have played out differently if I had taken fate into my own paws and escaped through the cat flap before David returned. I cannot honestly tell you why I didn't do so; why I decided instead to go back into Margery's bedroom, press myself up against the cold radiator and wait for whatever fate had in store for me. Maybe part of me still hoped that I would be taken to live with Margery in her new home. Or, if I'm being truthful, maybe I was just too frightened to go out into the world and fend for myself. I had enjoyed a life of comfortable privilege; let's face it, I was a pampered lap-cat. Courage and self-reliance were not qualities that I had ever been called upon to find within me. At least not yet.

Eventually the men had packed the bed and the last few boxes into the lorry and left. The house was silent once more, but it did not feel peaceful to me. It was an eerie kind of quiet, which set my teeth on edge. I meditated myself into a light doze on the bedroom floor, but even in sleep I could not rest. I dozed fitfully, dreaming that I could hear Margery calling my name, followed by a falling sensation, which jerked me back to consciousness as panic coursed through my body.

I heard a car pull up to the house. It was starting to get dark outside and the bedroom was chilly. The front door slammed, and I heard David sigh. He picked up the cat carrier in the hall and started to check the downstairs rooms, looking for me.

'Come on, you bloody cat. Where are you?' David called out, not bothering to hide the malice in his voice.

Even though I knew it was hopeless, my feline self-preservation instinct made me drop to my haunches and prowl around. I was looking for somewhere to hide, but with all the rooms empty, there was no shelter to be found.

As David got to the top of the stairs he saw me running back into Margery's bedroom and by the time he entered the room I was sitting on the windowsill, determined to meet him with my chin up and defiance in my eyes.

'All right, you, it's time to go,' he said, fiddling with the door of the cat carrier to unlock it. I began to growl again and, as he approached, I flattened my ears and pulled my top lip back in a hiss. He paused, wondering how best to handle me without getting his hands lacerated, and I was gratified to see a flicker of fear cross his face. I increased the volume and intensity of my hissing, making the most of having some power over him.

He moved the cat carrier into his left hand and, while I was distracted, grabbed the scruff of my neck with his right hand. He shoved me roughly inside, swinging the door shut behind me.

I slipped on the plastic floor of the carrier, trying to find my footing as he swung me round and turned to leave the room. Still growling, I peered through the bars of the carrier door for one final look at my home. The rooms were all empty, devoid of furniture and packing boxes. I was surprised by how cold the house looked, how lifeless without Margery's possessions and the warmth of her presence. The only sign that she had ever lived there were marks on the carpet, where her furniture had stood, and nails in the walls where her pictures had hung. I tried not to think about the happy times we had had in the house, the meals we had eaten together and our leisurely cuddles on the sofa.

In a matter of seconds we were outside. I heard the front door slam behind me and the key turn in the lock. The cat carrier bumped against David's leg as he walked across the drive to his car. I was spun around once more and briefly blinded by the light from a lamp post. Then the carrier was plonked unceremoniously into the boot of the car, the door was pushed shut and all was dark and silent.

4

The engine revved into life, and I felt the car slide off Margery's driveway. In an effort to stay calm, I began to observe my surroundings, trying to ignore the hunger pangs telling me that it was almost my dinner time. I circled round and round inside the cat carrier, trying to find a position that allowed me to see the car's rear windscreen, but the deepening dusk outside meant that all I could make out was the strobing flash of street lamps. Eventually, realizing anything else was futile, I crouched down on the floor of the carrier, with my feet tucked neatly underneath my body, and tried to let the hum and vibration of the engine lull me to sleep.

I must have fallen into a light doze, for I was woken by an incessant bleeping noise from the front of the car that I recognized as David's mobile phone. I heard David swear.

'Pat, I'm driving. Hang on – I'll put you on hands-free.'

I could make out the tinny sound of a woman's voice on the line. I had met David's wife Pat on a few occasions, back when she and David used to come for Sunday lunch at Margery's with their children. She had struck me as a pleasant woman, if somewhat worn down by the demands of two boisterous children and a husband whose emotional level seemed permanently set to 'stressed'.

'How's Mum doing?' David asked.

'She's not too bad. We've unpacked and she's having a cup of tea in the residents' lounge. You know what she's like, though, how she gets fixated on things. She keeps asking about the cat, wanting to know when you'll be bringing her.'

My heart leapt with excitement. Could this whole horrendous ordeal be about to end with an ecstatic reunion at Margery's new home?

David tutted loudly.

'For God's sake, I've been through this a million times with her. I've explained that she can't have pets there. She knows that.'

'I know, David,' Pat answered, her tone placatory. 'I've reminded her of that today as well. She nods, like she's taking it in, but I don't know if she's really understood.' There was a short silence before she added,

'I've put a photo of the cat on her bedside table, next to the photo of your dad, but I'm not sure if that's just going to make her worse.'

I felt as if my heart was going to burst with sorrow. Not for myself, and the crushing disappointment that we were not to be reunited after all, but for Margery. To think of her in strange surroundings, scared and confused – not just wanting but *needing* me – was almost more than I could bear.

David groaned. 'Maybe it will – how should I know? Hopefully she'll settle down soon and forget all about the bloody cat. I dunno, Pat. As if it wasn't stressful enough having to rehome my mother, now I've got to rehome her sodding cat too!'

Inside the plastic carrier, my fur bristled.

'I'm on my way to Rob's now, to drop her off. I've told Rob I owe him a pint for taking her,' David added, and my ears pricked up. I had never heard of Rob before, but by the sound of it, he was to be my new owner.

David finished the phone call and the rest of the journey passed in silence. I tried to keep track of how long we had been driving. I could see it was dark outside now and, judging from the ache in my stomach, it was at least an hour past my dinner time. Occasionally I let out a yowl, which was met with a curt 'Shut up, cat!' from the front seat, so after a while I gave up.

Eventually I felt the car slow down and pull to a halt. I instinctively burrowed as far back inside the carrier as I could, trying to make myself as small and inconspicuous as possible. The rational part of me knew it was pointless to try and hide, but my self-preservation instinct kicked in nonetheless.

I heard David get out of the car, slamming the door behind him. With my nose pressed against the back wall of the carrier, I listened to the sounds outside. The creak of a gate opening, David's footsteps on a path, then a door knocker being rapped twice. My fur stood on end as the knocking was swiftly followed by barking.

Trying to ignore my thumping heartbeat, I focused on attempting to discern how many different barks I could hear. It sounded like three: one deep and power-ful bark, plus two higher-pitched, yappier ones. Before I had time to visualize what kind of dogs might pro-duce such noises, the car boot was flung open. I felt someone grab the carrier's handle and yank it out of the car so roughly that I lost my footing and slid across the floor, so that my rear end was pressed against the bars at the front. I quickly spun round, bracing myself to face my next trauma head-on.

As I was carried up the path I heard David say, 'Cheers, mate. You're really helping me out here.'

We were now inside a front hall, and I had been placed on the doormat. Suddenly there seemed to be dogs everywhere, charging at me from all sides. The plastic carrier offered some protection, but I could see noses and slobbering mouths trying to press through the bars at the front, and countless legs seemed to pace around as they tried to find a way to get to me. The dogs' stale, smelly breath filled the carrier, making me want to retch. My back was arched and I hissed and spat with every ounce of my being, trying to warn my tormentors to back off.

'She'll have to get used to the dogs,' a man's voice – presumably Rob's – said, somewhat apologetically. That, I thought ruefully, was an understatement. 'We used to have a cat, so they should be okay with her,' he went on hopefully, but, to my mind, not very convincingly, 'although Nancy did disappear, after I got Stan. One minute she was hissing at him from the top of the fridge, the next minute she'd vanished into thin air – never came back. The vet was quite cross with me about that,' he added with a sigh, evidently dwelling on the injustice of being blamed for the previous cat's disappearance.

Every hair on my body was standing on end, and I'm ashamed to admit that any concern for Margery's fate had gone from my mind. My only thought was the realization that I was about to be left in a house with three dogs. Dogs with a track record of forcing cats to run away.

5

From the relative safety of my cat carrier, I observed my canine tormentors. The largest was stockily built with muscular shoulders and a barrel chest. His square, jowly face and wide-set eyes lent a dim-witted quality to his appearance, but there was no mistaking his strength as he barged against the carrier, trying to root me out of my hiding place. The other two dogs were identical-looking scrappy creatures, with over-sized, pointed ears. They were hardly any bigger than me, so I had a good view of their beady eyes and tiny white teeth, which were bared in a snarl.

When Rob flung the carrier door open I launched myself across the hallway so fast that my paws skidded on the floorboards and I almost ended up flat on my back. My strategy paid off, however, and my sudden departure took the dogs by surprise. The small ones barked shrilly as I streaked passed them, while the big jowly dog seemed baffled, and as I flew around the corner into the front room he was still sniffing at the cat carrier, wondering where I had gone.

On first glance, the front room offered few escape routes. My instincts were telling me to find high ground, so I leapt onto the sofa, springboarding from its back onto a dresser by the window. My paws skidded on a pile of magazines and I almost fell to the floor, but just managed to scrabble my way back, before leaping up to the top of a bookcase.

Trying not to inhale the dust that surrounded me, I lay down and tucked my legs under my body, taking in the view of Rob's living room from my aerial platform. Its focal point seemed to be an enormous television suspended from the wall, towards which all the seats in the room were facing. Other than piles of magazines and remote controls on a coffee table, there were very few personal possessions. I compared my surroundings with my memories of Margery's house, with its cosy clutter of polished photo frames and ornaments arranged on lacy cloths. The two sofas here were shiny and smooth, nothing like Margery's invitingly cushioned ones.

The dogs had followed my scent trail and were now in the room with me. I observed silently as each one moved around the floor methodically, sniffing the furniture in an attempt to work out where I had gone.

I maintained my sphinx-like pose high up on the bookcase while they trawled the room, becoming increasingly frustrated by their failure to hunt me down. Eventually they lost interest, leaving the room one by one, and as my adrenaline rush began to subside, I curled into a ball and fell asleep.

I was woken by a loud rumbling noise that made my whole body shake. My first thought was of the removal lorry, and for a confused few seconds I wondered whether I was about to be moved again. Then I realized that the sound was coming from the television. I looked across and noticed Rob sprawled across the sofa, a remote control in one hand and a large bowl of crisps in the other. He was shovelling crisps into his mouth by the handful, washing them down with sips from a can, which he placed on the arm of the sofa. He was completely absorbed in watching cars racing around a track on the screen, and every now and then he emitted a yelp of excitement or annoyance. Quizzically I observed him, wondering what he found enthralling about such a monotonous, noisy form of entertainment. His trance-like state was broken only when he opened his mouth to belch loudly.

I averted my eyes in disgust and began to wash.

It was not possible to imagine an owner more different from Margery. Everything about Margery had been gentle, careful and quiet. Rob was uncouth, noisy and messy. I thought longingly of the afternoons spent curled up on Margery's sofa watching television programmes about antiques, or gentle quiz shows. Try as I might, I could not envisage a time when I would be curled up on Rob's lap, happily watching his ear-splitting racing cars.

And then, of course, there were the dogs.

As I had been washing, one of the small rat-like dogs had wandered into the room and, noticing movement on top of the bookcase, had started to bark demonically at me. Soon rat-dog number two had run in to see what all the fuss was about, followed by the muscular square-faced dog. It didn't take long for them to spot me in my lofty hideout and soon they were all barking, their cacophonous racket drowning out the droning engines onscreen.

'Oi, you three, that's enough!'

Roused into action, Rob spun round, grappling for something to hurl at the dogs. He grabbed a magazine and flung it in their general direction, but as it flew through the air the magazine clipped the drink can balanced on the sofa's arm. The can rocked from side to side before toppling over the side of the sofa, spraying its contents across the carpet and over the dogs. Rob roared an expletive as he dived over the side of the sofa to retrieve the can from the floor. Doing his best to siphon the still-fizzing contents into his mouth, he sat back down on the sofa, upending the bowl of crisps, which he had left in the middle of his seat.

I paused mid-wash and allowed a wry smile to spread across my lips.

Rob growled and made a cursory attempt to sweep the loose crisps from the sofa cushions back into the bowl, before storming out of the room to fetch a cloth. The dogs, sensing his anger, beat a hasty retreat into another room.

In the days that followed, I began, reluctantly, to adjust to life in Rob's house. I studied the dogs' behaviour, observing when they went for their walks and when they slept, and tailored my own sleeping pattern so that our waking hours coincided as little as possible. I learnt what triggered their rage: the little rat-like dogs went into a barking frenzy whenever the doorbell rang, whereas the big dog was driven to the point of apo-plexy if anyone went near his food bowl while he was eating.

Stan, the square-faced dog, was without a doubt an intimidating beast, but thankfully he was not the clev-erest of animals. If he saw me walking anywhere in the vicinity of his food bowl he would growl ominously, but he was easily confused by my feline agility, and my habit of leaping upwards and disappearing out of sight constantly left him baffled.

It was Chas and Dave, the little dogs, that I soon realized posed more of a problem for me. I had considered them a single entity, as they always did everything together. In actual fact, I couldn't tell them apart. They egged each other on in their malice towards me. Their favourite sport was to chase me into a corner of the house from which it was impossible to escape, and then bark maniacally so that my hair stood on end and my tail had fluffed out to double its usual size. I would hiss and spit in retaliation, and we would remain in this three-way stand-off until a momentary lapse in the dogs' concentration afforded me a split-second chance to dash to safety, streaking past them and up onto higher ground, from where I would eye them contemptuously.

Not surprisingly, I began to spend more time outside than I had ever done at Margery's. Up until now I'd always considered myself more an indoor cat; I had generally felt nervous stepping outside the quiet safety of Margery's house. But Rob's house did not feel quiet or safe to me, so in desperation I began to take refuge in the garden.

At first I would sit on the fence post, too nervous to venture beyond my immediate vicinity. Looking down the row of back gardens, I could see that I was surrounded on all sides by houses exactly like Rob's. Each had a neat rectangle of lawn at the back, which was edged by fencing. Some lawns were pristine and trimmed, others were sparse and patchy with trampolines or goalposts in the middle of them. Overall the street had a busier, noisier feel to it than Margery's cul-de-sac. There were more children, more dogs and the constant noise of music, or of balls being kicked against walls.

One of Rob's neighbours had an elderly tomcat, who spent the days sunning himself on the patio of his back garden. He would eye me suspiciously if I strayed into his territory. I would chirrup a friendly 'good morning' to him, but he never did any more than harrumph in reply. Further down the street there was a pair of young cats, not long out of kittenhood. Just watching them tearing up and down trees or flinging themselves at every bird that landed in their garden left me feeling exhausted.

The cat who most intrigued me was a small black cat with lively green eyes, who I often saw trotting past the front of Rob's house. I couldn't work out where she lived, as she always seemed to be coming and going from different houses, but she had a happy air and confident demeanour, which I envied. She sometimes noticed me watching her, but always seemed so focused on whatever she was doing that I never felt confident enough to stop her and talk.

In the early hours of the morning when everyone

else was asleep, I would reflect on my new life, and on the life I had lost. I berated myself for not appreciating how lucky I had been when I lived with Margery. If I had known then what I knew now, perhaps I would have done things differently. Maybe I could have done more to help Margery and to prevent the calamity that was to befall us both. Was my natural complacency to blame? If I had been a better cat, perhaps none of this would have happened. Whether or not I was right to blame myself, I had to accept the reality of my new life: it was simply an existence, a succession of daily obstacles to be overcome. There was no love or affection in my life any more, for Rob took very little interest in me and the feeling was mutual.

The thought did cross my mind that there was nothing stopping me from leaving, but where would I go? Life with Rob and the dogs had very little to recommend it, but I did at least have food and shelter. What was the alternative? I was not yet ready to take my chances and find out.

6

As the days turned to weeks, Chas and Dave continued to bait me at every opportunity, and after a while I accepted that their high-pitched yapping was a constant background accompaniment to my life. Rob, on the other hand, seemed to have forgotten that I existed. When he remembered he would put a bowl of dry food down for me, and would shout at the dogs if he saw them lunge at me, but other than that he barely interacted with me at all.

It would be an exaggeration to say that I had settled into my new home, but as time went on there was a certain familiarity to the routine of it. I had stopped thinking about Margery so much, and no longer lulled myself to sleep by remembering her lavender scent and imagining the feel of her hand stroking my fur. I tried my hardest to live in the present, and neither to dwell on the past nor worry about the future. I faced each day as its own challenge, and hoped that I would make it to night-time with minimal aggravation from the dogs. Perhaps life would have carried on like that, and I might still be there now, if it hadn't been for Stan and the dog biscuit.

Stan was as an all-mouth-and-no-trousers kind of dog. He could look terrifying, with his muscles tensed and his wide eyes bulging, but behind his brawny exterior there was very little in the way of brains. Over time, I started to get complacent around him, feeling confident that I could easily outwit him.

One afternoon when I was in the kitchen I heard the front door open – Rob was back from walking the dogs. I jumped onto the kitchen counter in anticipation, knowing from experience that Rob always fed the dogs after their walk. I hoped that, if I sat in the middle of the worktop, Rob would remember to feed me as well.

He poured out the meaty biscuits into three bowls and placed them on the kitchen floor. The kitchen filled with the sounds of snorting and chomping as the dogs devoured their food. As usual, I observed their slovenly manners with an air of disgust. Stan finished first, pushing the bowl across the kitchen floor as he licked every last crumb from the dish. Satisfied that there was nothing left to eat, he sniffed the bowl, then walked across the kitchen to drop himself into his wicker basket. Rob had gone into the front room and I could hear the television blaring. Not for the first time, he had forgotten to put out my food.

Chas and Dave were busy wolfing down their biscuits, so I took the opportunity to jump down to the floor and slip silently past them, to make my way quickly up the hall. The front-room door was closed, but I could hear the din of the television within. I hoped Rob would realize he had forgotten about me, but my scratching and mewing couldn't be heard over the noise from the TV. My tummy was rumbling, and the injustice of seeing the dogs fill their faces while I was left to starve irritated me. I padded back into the kitchen. Stan was washing his hindquarters in his basket; Chas and Dave were chomping in unison, with their backs to me.

My stomach growled with hunger, so I tiptoed over to Stan's bowl and cautiously sniffed at it. I could make out the faint trace of a meaty smell of biscuit underneath the bowl. The challenge of how to reach the biscuit absorbed me, and when I realized that I couldn't get to it by nudging the bowl with my nose, I tried with my paw instead, hoping to catch the rim of the bowl with my claws and lift it off the floor long enough to swipe the biscuit out.

My first couple of attempts were fruitless, the bowl slipping from my claws before I could lift it, so on my third attempt I was more assertive. I felt the rim of the bowl catch on my claws and, with my nose to the floor, slid my other paw under the dish. I could see the biscuit, tantalizingly just out of reach. Extending my claws, I tried desperately to make contact with the biscuit, but just when I thought it was within my grasp, my grip slipped and the bowl crashed down noisily on the kitchen tiles.

An eerie silence filled the kitchen, as the sound of canine chomping came to an abrupt end. Glancing over my shoulder, I saw all three dogs staring at me, their mouths open in disbelief. Stan had been washing his nether-regions in his basket and had stopped mid-lick, hind legs akimbo, his eyes flicking from me to his food bowl and back again. It was as if I could hear his thought processes: That cat has been trying to eat *my* food. From *my* bowl. *While I am in the room.*

Before I had a chance to leap to safety, Stan shot out of his bed and charged at me. Chas and Dave erupted into a barking frenzy, jumping up and down and trembling with excitement.

What happened next felt like a blur. I heard the scrape of claws on tile – whether Stan's or mine, I'm not sure – and saw Stan's rage-filled face looming towards me, teeth bared and ready to bite. Dim-witted he may have been, but I was in no doubt that at that moment he intended to rip me limb from limb. I heard Chas and Dave's hysterical yapping as they egged Stan on, delighted that he was about to deliver some canine justice. That was when something inside me snapped. Without thinking, I turned to face Stan and launched myself, legs outstretched and claws bared, at his glistening nose and slobbery mouth.

I was aware that the room had fallen silent again, as Chas and Dave watched me soar above their heads, a furry, four-legged missile. I landed perfectly on target, my claws making contact with Stan's muzzle. I felt his flesh – surprisingly soft, given its muscly appearance – yield under my razor-sharp grip. My hind legs swung underneath me as I hung on to Stan's face with all my might. Meanwhile my ears were pinned back against my head and I hissed and spat with all the ferocity I could muster. All the injustices of the previous few weeks seemed to come to a head in that split-second encounter: my rage at David for taking Margery, and my home, away from me; my anger at Rob for taking me on, when he clearly didn't care about me at all; and my fury at the dogs for making my life miserable.

After a brief, stunned silence, Chas and Dave redoubled their barking and Stan produced a noise that I have never heard from a dog before or since: a yelp crossed with a shriek, at a pitch far higher than his normal vocal range. As the surge of adrenaline and rage that had got me thus far began to subside, I realized, with not a small sense of panic, that my claws had sunk so far into Stan's face that I was having difficulty retracting them. The fact that my entire body weight was hanging suspended from my front paws probably didn't help. I pumped my back feet, trying to make contact with his chest, thinking that if I could just push my body a little higher I would be able to withdraw my claws, but as I kicked out at him, Stan started to walk backwards in an attempt to shield himself from this second onslaught.

After what felt like an eternity, Rob was roused by the commotion and flung the kitchen door open.

'What the bloody hell is going on in here?' he shouted at Chas and Dave, before pausing to look, aghast, at Stan and me. We were still locked in our vicious embrace, my back legs frantically kicking, and Stan now shaking his head from side to side in a desperate but futile attempt to dislodge me.

'What the—?' Rob muttered in disbelief. Then he let out a roar of laughter, which set Chas and Dave barking again. 'That cat's a frickin' ninja!' he hooted, pulling his phone out of his pocket and pointing it at us, to film the scene of carnage.

Perhaps it was the humiliation of being laughed at

that did it: Stan gave one final, decisive twist of his head, which was powerful enough to shake me free, although not without ripping a strip of flesh from his muzzle. He yelped like a puppy and ran whimpering out of the room, while I sprang up onto the kitchen table and from there leapt to safety on top of the fridge.

Rob put his phone back in his pocket and returned to the front room, chortling to himself. Chas and Dave ran after him, still wired with excitement. My heart was racing, so I started to wash, trying to calm myself down. Part of me felt elated at having triumphed over the dogs so spectacularly. But another part of me felt ashamed at what I had become: a vicious animal, no better than the brute of a dog I had attacked. I tried hard to lick the scent of Stan off my paws. What would Margery have thought, if she had seen me behave in such a way? The Molly she knew would never bare her claws to anyone, let alone pick a fight with a dog like Stan. I had proved a point to the dogs, but at what cost to my dignity?

I closed my eyes and thought about Margery, trying to remember the kind of cat I had been when I lived with her. Pampered – undoubtedly; spoilt – probably; but I had been also been gentle, affectionate and caring. Since I had lost Margery, I seemed to have lost that part of myself as well, and I didn't like what I was turning into. I cleaned myself thoroughly from nose to tail, trying to wash away the cat that I had become. When I had finished washing I felt calm, and I curled up on the top of the fridge. As my mind began to drift I imagined Margery's voice saying, 'It will all be better after a good night's sleep.' I started to purr and allowed myself to sink into the silent blackness, knowing that when I woke up I would have a decision to make.

I opened my eyes, feeling instantly alert. The kitchen was silent apart from the ticking of the wall clock and the first notes of the birds' dawn chorus outside. The room was bathed in grey light, and through the window I could see the first flecks of pink and gold in the sky. I saw the dogs' food bowls on the floor and winced, as the events of the previous evening flooded back into my mind. I jumped down onto the floor and stretched, noticing the lone dog biscuit that had been the cause of so much drama. In the fracas it had got kicked across the room, landing next to the bin. In the absence of anything else for breakfast, I ate it, resolute that this would be my last meal in Rob's house.

When I had finished I slipped quietly through the cat flap and stood on the patio, my tail twitching as I considered my options. Although there was very little I would miss about this house, I was not naive – I knew there was no certainty I would find anything better elsewhere. Still, I promised myself that I would not settle for second best. The next place I called home would be somewhere I could be the kind of cat I wanted to be: a cat who would make Margery proud.

7

I made my way down the side of the house, slipped under the garden gate onto the pavement and started walking. The streets were empty and the houses were dark, their residents still sleeping. It had been almost twenty-four hours since my last meal, so breakfast was a pressing concern. Fortunately dawn was the perfect hour for hunting, and it didn't take me long to find a shrew scurrying underneath a hedge.

As the sun rose, the neighbourhood began to come to life. It was a crisp autumn morning. The sun was bright but not yet warm, and a cool breeze whipped the fallen leaves into flurries along the pavement. I watched as people rushed from their houses, slamming their front doors behind them, before jumping into their cars. I knew that it was not too late to change my mind: I could turn around, go back to Rob's house and carry on as before, as if nothing had happened. But my resolve was firm, and I was certain that I would not be dissuaded from my plan, even if I wasn't sure yet what that plan was.

I padded along the pavement, crossing roads and turning corners at random, with no conscious purpose other than to keep moving. Eventually, I arrived at a small children's playground at the outskirts of Rob's housing estate. Although I could not have been walking for much more than an hour, I was beginning to feel weary, and the expanse of soft grass in the empty playground looked inviting. I squeezed under the iron gate and made my way towards the sunniest corner of the playground, beyond a row of swings. As I got closer, I realized there was already a cat there, washing.

'Hello,' I called. 'Do you mind if I join you?'

The cat jumped slightly at the sound of my voice, but I was relieved to see that her expression when she turned to look at me was friendly.

'I'm Molly,' I said, by way of introduction.

As I got closer I recognized the black cat with green eyes who I had seen around the neighbourhood.

'Hello, Molly. Be my guest,' she replied.

I sat down next to her and closed my eyes, enjoying the warmth of the sun on my face. She continued to wash, and we sat in comfortable silence for a few minutes.

'I've seen you around. You're new to the neighbour-hood, aren't you?' she asked.

I opened my eyes. 'Yes, I've been here a few weeks. Got rehomed here. Don't think I'm staying, though,' I added.

The black cat looked at me and I detected a smile in her eyes. 'Let me guess. Three dogs: one muscle-bound dunce and two psychotic midgets. Am I right?'

I looked at her open-mouthed. 'Yes, how did you . . . ?'

'I'm Nancy.'

I stared at her, trying to place the name. It took me a moment, but suddenly I was transported back to David's car, overhearing Rob talking about a previous cat who had disappeared, scared off by the dogs. Nancy had been her name, I was sure of it.

'Are you – were you – did you live with Rob before?' I stammered.

'Correct,' she replied, before wrinkling her nose in distaste at the memory. 'I was wondering how long you'd last,' she added conspiratorially.

'Did you know I was there?' I asked, disconcerted to think she had been observing me for all this time.

'I was keeping an eye on you, of course. Why do you think you kept bumping into me on the street? You seemed to be coping admirably, so I thought it better not to get involved.'

I wasn't sure how I felt about this revelation, so I said nothing.

'So where do you live now?' I asked after a few moments. 'Rob said you ran away and he never saw you again.'

Nancy narrowed her eyes ruefully. 'I don't think he *looked* very hard for me. But I'm still around, as you can see.'

'So, who's your new owner?' My heart surged with excitement – perhaps Nancy's new owner might have room for another of Rob's refuseniks.

Nancy took a deep breath and her brow furrowed. 'You know what – I'm not sure that I'm okay with this whole "owner" concept. It doesn't pay to be dependent on one human. Just look at what happens if you end up with one like Rob, for instance.'

I tilted my head in acknowledgement.

'My current arrangement is rather more . . . liberal, you could say.'

'So, you don't have a home? Are you a stray?' I wasn't sure if I liked the sound of Nancy's 'liberal arrangement'.

Nancy looked horrified. 'A stray! Of course not. I have several homes – it's just that none of them are . . . exclusive.' She shot me a mischievous look, then started to lick one of her front paws.

'Oh, okay,' I replied, wondering whether such an

arrangement would suit me. 'So how many homes do you have?'

She paused mid-wash and stared into the middle distance, as if counting in her head. 'Probably around six at the moment,' she said nonchalantly. 'Give or take a couple.'

She glanced at me, amused by my look of confusion.

'You get to take your pick of where to eat, where to sleep, who to spend time with,' she explained. 'No commitments, no responsibilities. It's a good deal – you should try it.'

I tried to picture myself living like that, trotting between streets from one home to another, deciding on a whim which owner to grace with my presence that evening.

'Hmm, I'm not sure. It sounds kind of fun, but I think I'm a one-owner kind of cat, really.'

'Fair enough,' Nancy replied amiably. 'Each to their own.'

She carried on cleaning her paw while I sat, deep in thought.

'So what was the final straw then? At Rob's? What made you leave?' she asked.

Fortunately cats' blushes aren't visible through their fur, but I could feel my face burn as the degrading spectacle of me swinging from Stan's jowls came into my mind.

'Oh, well, I tried to eat one of the dogs' biscuits—'
I began, sheepishly.

'Which dog?' Nancy interjected.

'Stan,' I answered.

She winced and sucked through her teeth.

'And then he went for me and I kind of . . . lost it.'

Nancy was looking at me intently, clearly delighting
in the vicarious experience of exacting revenge on her
old foe. She nodded at me to continue.

'So I sort of . . .' I tried to recreate my pose as I had
launched myself at Stan: forelegs stretched out, claws
bared.

Nancy's eyes widened.

'And then I kind of . . . flew. At his nose.'

She squeaked with delight.

'But then I found I was sort of . . . stuck. On his
face.' I mimed myself hanging from my front paws.

Nancy's reaction made me see the funny side of the
episode for the first time, and I started to enjoy telling
the story.

'He tried to shake me off, but couldn't, because I was
kicking him in the chest.' I pumped my back legs
against the ground to demonstrate.

'He eventually shook me off, but I took a fair chunk
of his face with me.'

'That. Is. Brilliant,' she said approvingly. 'I *wish* I
had been there to see it.'

'It didn't really feel brilliant at the time, but Rob seemed to find it hilarious.'

We sat side by side, intermittently washing and comparing experiences of life with Rob and his dogs.

'So where do you think I should go then, to find a new owner?' I asked at last. 'I don't want to stay around here.' The thought of Rob finding me and taking me back to his house or, even worse, calling David to come and get me did not bear thinking about.

Nancy lifted her chin and looked around thoughtfully.

'I suppose the best thing might be to head for town. I think it's just a few miles that way.' She jerked her head in the direction of the main road which ran alongside the playground. 'There will be plenty of potential owners there, I'm sure of it. Although maybe you should spend a few days with me, before you set off,' she added. 'I can give you a few pointers. You don't strike me as a cat who's had to fend for herself before.'

I had to concede that she was right, and I gratefully accepted her offer.

Over the next few days I stuck close to Nancy as she shared her survival tips, such as how to sneak in through cat flaps to steal other cats' food, and how to scavenge from dustbins. She showed me how to find overnight shelter, and how to cross busy roads safely.

I eagerly absorbed everything she told me, secretly hoping I wouldn't ever be called upon to use these skills.

She also taught me what she called her feline–human management strategy. It had never occurred to me to have a strategy in my relations with humans – to me, it was a straightforward case of find an owner you love and hope they love you back.

'Humans always think they know what they want,' Nancy explained, 'but they don't always know what they *need*. That's where a cat comes in. You can be the one to show them.'

I wasn't sure I understood what she meant, but I nodded eagerly nonetheless.

At last Nancy seemed satisfied that I was capable of surviving on my wits alone, and we set off early one morning for the playground at the edge of the estate.

'Town's that way,' she said, looking north along the main road. 'Stick to the hedgerows. There should be plenty of wildlife in there to keep you going, and farms along the way. And don't cross this road unless you absolutely have to,' she added with a look of sincere concern.

I nodded.

'You know you can always come back, if things don't work out. I'll be here. I'm sure we could find you a home, or six.'

Her offer touched me, and for the first time I felt a twinge of disquiet about what lay ahead. Was I doing the right thing? I wondered. I may not have found an owner, but I had found a friend. Was I crazy to be leaving Nancy behind and setting out for an uncertain future in some unknown town?

As if she'd read my mind Nancy said, 'You'll be fine, I know it. You've been trained by the best, after all.'

She blinked at me and then leant forward. We touched noses briefly, a fleeting gesture that we both knew meant goodbye.

'Well, go on then – off you go!' she said, feigning impatience.

'Thank you,' I stuttered. Feeling my eyes start to prickle, I turned away. I slipped under the playground gate and across the grassy verge to the hedgerow that ran parallel to the road. I turned and looked at Nancy, who was watching me intently, her tail erect in salutation. I lifted my tail to mirror her posture, before turning to face the track ahead of me, ready to take my first steps as an independent cat.

8

Heeding Nancy's words, I stayed close to the hedgerow that bordered the road, keeping well clear of the cars that roared past. Before long, Rob's housing estate had disappeared behind a dip in the road and I was in open countryside.

My days quickly developed a rhythm. I hunted at dawn and dusk, walked during the daylight hours and found shelter overnight in the hedgerows and stone walls that criss-crossed the adjacent fields. My paw pads were soon sore from the constant walking, my legs ached, and I felt permanently exhausted. Having always considered washing to be an aid to meditation as much as a physical necessity, it was a shock to realize that a thorough top-to-toe wash was now a daily essential to remove the mud and burrs my fur had picked up. I was surprised, however, to find that I slept better in the open air than I ever had in Rob's house. In spite of being exposed to the elements, my physical exertion meant that I slept deeply and soundly, from the moment I closed my eyes, until the sound of the dawn birdsong woke me.

Outdoor life was tiring and uncomfortable, but in those early days it was also exhilarating. Over time, my physical stamina improved and my hunting technique, which had always been somewhat half-hearted, was honed to brutal efficiency. I also became familiar with the natural world in a way that had never been necessary as an indoor cat. My knowledge of birds had been limited to those I could see from my windowsill – I had never troubled myself to wonder where they nested, or what they ate. Now I was learning that certain hedges were guaranteed to attract the songbirds that loved to feast on their berries, and I could be sure of a kill if I lurked, motionless, nearby. I could also tell from the reactions of the smaller birds when a bird of prey was hovering above the trees at the side of the road, a useful indicator that small rodents were in the vicinity.

The only signs of human habitation that I encountered were farm buildings. I would make a detour from my track to walk over to them – a night spent in a hay-filled barn felt like luxury, compared to what I had become used to. If I encountered people I would keep my head down and dart behind a wall or a piece of machinery. They would ignore me, assuming I was a farm cat, and I was happy to let them do so.

I had lost count of the number of days that had gone by since leaving the estate. My awareness of time's passing came from the changes in light and air temperature. I had rarely felt cold when I had set out, and the sunlight had felt warm on my back. As the days had gone by, I was aware that the sun was rising lower in the sky and that its pale rays no longer exuded any warmth. The wind cut through my fur, and when it rained I was forced to seek shelter, otherwise a chill would soak through to my bones, leaving me shivery and weak. I knew that winter was coming, and for the first time I felt a flutter of panic. I didn't know how far I was from town, but I would have to reach it before the depths of winter set in. I knew I could not survive outdoors once the months of snow and frost arrived.

One damp, grey afternoon I allowed my mind to wander as I plodded along the muddy track. I had tried not to let myself think about Margery since setting off for the town, but in my downcast mood I summoned up memories of winters at her house. There had been a rug on the floor in front of the gas fire, where I would doze for hours, legs outstretched and belly exposed, stirring only to change position when the heat became too much and I would turn so that a different part of my body faced the flames. I couldn't help but wonder if I would ever find another home like Margery's.

In the distance, through the drizzle, I could see what looked like a farm: a cluster of low buildings facing each other across a yard. I began to head towards it with some relief: it had felt like a long day and I was looking forward to a good wash and a nap under a barn roof. Tired though I was, I picked up my pace to a trot. As I reached the grassy verge outside the farm's entrance, I looked up at the wooden sign painted in a sloping, cursive script: 'Cotswold Organic'. I peered around the stone pillar at the entrance gate. I saw a tarmacked car park, in which there was not a tractor or trailer to be seen, but rather rows of large cars with tinted glass windows, all of them spotlessly clean. My whiskers twitched with confusion.

I sniffed the air, and instead of the usual sour smell of animal dung and rotting hay I detected the delicious scents of fresh fish and cooked meats. My stomach lurched with hunger and my mouth started to salivate at the thought of prepared food, after my recent diet of rodents and birds. I slipped through the entrance gate and across the car park towards the complex of lime-washed wooden buildings arranged around a flagstone courtyard.

I paused at the edge of the car park. This definitely wasn't like any other farm I'd come across. It was too clean, and there was a stone fountain tinkling delicately in the middle of the yard. A wooden signpost to my right pointed variously to 'The Spa', 'Cookery School' and 'Farm Shop'. The sign indicated that the building on my left was the farm shop, so I tiptoed across to peer through its glazed doors. I was startled when the glass doors slid apart and a woman strode out, practically knocking me off my feet with the hessian shopping bag that was slung over her arm.

Before the doors could shut, I dashed inside and hid in the nearest place I could find: underneath a wooden trestle table piled high with fruit and vegetables. I felt relieved to be out of the cold and wet; savouring the feeling of warm air on my damp fur, from heaters above the door. I could see the legs of customers as they moved slowly around the shop floor, although the only sounds were polite murmurings from aproned members of staff as they wrapped items in tissue paper and placed them into large paper bags.

I wondered whether Margery had ever shopped at such a place as this. I remembered how, before her confusion, she had loved to cook fresh meat and fish for us both. The thought crossed my mind that there could be someone like Margery here, someone who might not be averse to taking a friendly – albeit soggy – cat home with their food shopping.

I crept forward and peered out from underneath the

table. The customers I could see were all female, but they looked very different from Margery. They were younger, and their clothes seemed to be variations on a theme: tight-fitting jeans, leather boots, padded gilets and long, glossy hair. I watched them as they moved around the displays, picking items from the shelves and studying them, before either dropping them into leather shopping baskets or placing them back on the shelf. I tried to imagine the houses they lived in, and to picture myself in them. But my frame of reference was limited to Margery's and Rob's homes, and somehow I couldn't see any of these women in houses like theirs.

I remained in my hiding place while I considered my options. I could make my way around the back of the building to scavenge in the bins for scraps, or I could try something more ambitious.

A customer was standing in front of the fruit and vegetable display, unwittingly dangling her leather shopping-basket about six inches from my nose. As she handled some of the produce on the table above me, I tiptoed forward and inhaled deeply. I could smell cheese, prawns and white fish, and my mouth began to water. The lady dropped some vegetables into the bag and then made her way towards the till.

Having paid for her shopping, she walked back across the shop to the exit. I darted out from under the table and followed, slipping through the automatic doors after her. I crossed the courtyard a few paces behind her, feeling excited and nervous, wondering if this could be the opportunity I had longed for: the moment I found my next owner.

She rummaged in her handbag for her car key and pointed it at a large, expensive-looking car, which bleeped in response. I was just about to begin my charm offensive, when she swung the boot open and a dog leapt out. Instantly, my tail fluffed out and I hissed as memories of Stan, Chas and Dave rushed into my mind. The dog was attached to the car by a leash, but that didn't stop him straining against it so hard that his eyes bulged. The woman turned round and, for the first time, noticed me.

'Urgh, where did that stray cat come from?' she said, her face contorted in revulsion.

This was not going according to plan. I had intended to mew piteously at this point, and to rub my head endearingly around her boots. Instead my ears were pinned back against my head, my back was arched, every hair was standing on end. It was beginning to dawn on me that this scene was unlikely to have a happy ending.

'Stop it, Inca. Inside!' she instructed the dog, which, reluctantly but obediently, jumped back into the boot of the car.

She glared and waved a rolled-up umbrella at me as

if I were vermin. Defeated, I gave a final parting hiss before breaking into a run through the car park and out onto the grassy verge.

Back on the muddy track, my annoyance gave way to disappointment. I had not had much time to dwell on my loneliness since making the decision to set off for town, but seeing the customers in the farm shop had given me a pang that felt like homesickness – a longing for a home, and an owner to call my own. Not just someone to protect and feed me, but someone whose face would light up when I walked into the room, who would be delighted if I jumped onto their lap for a cuddle. My life as a solitary, wandering cat was so different from my previous existence that I had almost forgotten what it felt like to be a pet, and to feel loved. My experience at the farm shop had reminded me that the world of humans and their houses, with their cosy kitchens and open fires, was still out there, but seemingly further out reach than ever.

Trying not to let self-pity swamp me, I trudged along the verge. The rain had stopped, but there was no escaping the winter chill in the air now, and the watery sun was already setting in the sky. The mud under my paws was cold and beginning to set hard: a frosty night lay ahead.

I followed the curve of the road and looked up to see a long hill stretching ahead of me. I could make out the orange glow of street lamps at the top, and the distant silhouette of buildings and rooftops. I felt a tingle of excitement: this must be the town Nancy had talked of.

The wind seemed to cut through me as I plodded up the hill. Cars raced past, their headlights glistening on the wet asphalt, their drivers no doubt rushing to get home for the evening. When I saw a road sign that read 'Welcome to Stourton-on-the-Hill, historic market town', I felt a strange mixture of relief and nervousness. I knew nothing about this town, but had set my heart on it as the place where I would find a home and an owner. Now that I had finally arrived, the enormity of my challenge began to hit me.

The light was fading and it had started to drizzle again. Normally I would have taken this as my cue to stop, to find a nook in the side of a wall or a hollow tree trunk and curl up for the night. My paws were numb with cold, my fur was soaked through, and I was beginning to feel chilled to my bones. But I felt an urge to push on, to make it into town before nightfall.

At the outer edge of the town, I hopped up onto the pavement, feeling suddenly exposed and vulnerable as I passed between shops and parked cars. I paused outside a takeaway restaurant – the smell of spicy meat that wafted out of an air vent made me painfully aware of my hunger. Stepping forward to peer through the restaurant window, I jumped when I saw a wild-looking cat inside, staring at me with a look of panic in its eyes. Startled, I stepped away from the window, my heart racing with shock. Slowly, I crept forwards, approaching the glass for another look. This time, it took only a moment to confirm my worst suspicion: that the wild cat in the restaurant was, in fact, my own reflection looking back at me.

I stared at myself in the glass in disbelief. Where once I had had soft flesh, there was now lean muscle. I could see the knobbles of my spine protruding through my fur, which was dull and matted in places. But it was my face that most surprised me – my chin looked pointed and my eye sockets were hollow. I recoiled in horror, thinking that I looked just like a stray. My heart sank as I realized that was exactly what I had become.

At that moment a man came out of the restaurant clutching a paper bag full of food containers. I closed my eyes momentarily to savour the delicious aromas of lamb and chicken. The man pulled his jacket up over his head to shield himself from the rain, then broke into a run. His feet splashed through a puddle as he ran past me, soaking me with dirty water. I shook what I could off me, knowing that I needed a thorough wash. I also knew I would have to find somewhere to shelter before I could afford myself that luxury.

I heard church bells in the distance. They reminded me of the clock on Margery's fireplace: six chimes meant my dinner hour, and she was never late, placing my china dish in front of me with a 'There you go, lovie'. I would eat happily, knowing that once dinner was finished we would settle down for a cuddle on the sofa. She would stroke my back and talk to me as she watched television, and I would purr in reply. That was how it had been with Margery – a routine that had evolved between us, an innate understanding of what the other wanted and needed.

Was it possible that I would ever have that sort of relationship with another person? And, if such a person were out there somewhere, in Stourton-on-the-Hill, how was I to go about finding them?

9

The sky had darkened ominously and heavy droplets of rain pounded my back, but I knew I had to keep walking. My first priority was to eat, and then to find shelter for the night. I lowered my head and followed the sound of the church bells, hoping they would lead me to the centre of town. As I plodded along the pavement a man ran out of a shop in front of me, shaking his umbrella open and spraying me with rainwater. Startled, I darted into a doorway and shook the loose water from my fur. When I peered out, I saw shoppers rushing along the street, their faces hidden by hoods and umbrellas.

I ducked back into the doorway, allowing myself a brief respite from the rain. Rivulets of water gushed along the kerbside gutter a few feet away from me, the drains overflowing in the downpour. The rain bounced relentlessly off the rooftops and dripped from shop awnings onto the pavement. It sounded hard and unforgiving, not like the soft pattering noise of rain falling on fields or hedgerows. My fur was soaked through and my paws were numb with cold, although I knew I had no choice but to carry on, in spite of my discomfort.

I slipped out of the doorway and, avoiding the rain-splashed kerb, ran as fast as I could to the end of the street. My head remained bowed as I followed the pavement round a bend, at which point I stopped, my ears twitching as they detected a change in my surroundings. The intense, echoing quality of the rain in the narrow street had gone and I sensed that the town had opened up in front of me. I could hear human voices on all sides, car engines and the clanking of metal in the distance. Feeling an urge to seek cover and get my bearings, I dashed between the wheels of a parked car and twisted my body rapidly from side to side, flicking the loose water from my fur. A shiver was starting to spread through my bones and my instincts were telling me to wash and sleep, but I knew it was too risky to settle down here. Exhausted though I was, my mind vividly recalled the look on Nancy's face as she instructed me, 'Never. Ever. Sleep underneath a parked car. Got it?'

Night was falling fast and I could not afford to linger. I peered out from under the car bonnet. Up ahead, buildings of honey-coloured stone faced onto a handsome market square, their mismatched rooftops silhouetted against the steel-grey sky. In the square, traders were packing away their market stalls, dismantling poles and loading unsold stock into their vans. The shops were closing for the night, but there were still a few people on the streets, grim-faced and laden with bags. After so long away from human habitation, I struggled to take in the scene before me. But it was not the noisiness of the square, or the bustling activity of the market traders, that made me catch my breath – it was the lights. Everywhere I looked there were bulbs strung between lamp posts, cables of fairy lights snaking through window displays, and illuminated stars twinkling in doorways. On the far side of the square, white bulbs were wreathed around a large fir tree. There was no mistaking the signs all around me: Christmas was coming.

As the shock of this realization sank in, I was reminded afresh of the life I had lost. When I had lived with Margery, Christmas had been my favourite time of year. The first sign of it was the appearance of Margery's small artificial tree by the front-room window. I would sit on the windowsill next to its sparse, bare branches, waiting patiently while Margery rummaged in the understairs cupboard for the box of decorations. As soon as she placed it on the living-room floor I would jump down and dip my paw into the mound of baubles inside, delighting in the rattling sound they made as I tried to catch them with my claws.

Margery would remove ornaments from the box one by one and hang them carefully on the tree, while I lurked behind, waiting to bat them off the branches with my paw. Margery would chide me, 'Tsk, Molly!', but she smiled as she spoke and never made any attempt to stop me. Once the baubles were in place, she would pull a long string of tinsel from the box and I would pounce on it, wrestling with its rustling fronds until Margery tugged it out from underneath me, laughing. She would weave a string of coloured lights around the tree and place a sparkly star at the top, then would stand back to appraise her work. 'There, Molly, what do you think?' she would ask, and I would purr in approval.

I slid out from under the car now, feeling vulnerable and exposed as I began to skirt around the edge of the square. The market traders were oblivious to my presence as I slunk behind their vans. I glanced up at each shop I passed: their windows were full of antiques, cookware or walking boots and waxed jackets. A chalkboard on the pavement alerted me to the presence of a pub up ahead. Its door was open onto the street, inviting passers-by to take refuge from the chill and damp outside. I tiptoed into its wooden porch, glimpsing a cosy wooden-beamed bar and a roaring log fire inside. It was almost temptation beyond endurance, to see people warming their feet by the flames and not slip across the room to join them. But the aroma of damp dog hung in the air, and the 'Dogs welcome' sign on the door left me in no doubt that this was an establishment that favoured dogs over cats.

As I continued my circuit of the square, I passed a bookshop and an interior-design store with swathes of fabric draped across a chaise longue in the window. My stomach rumbled insistently, reminding me that I needed to find something to eat as a matter of urgency. I came across a bakery that proclaimed its 'organic artisan breads', but its shelves were empty and it was dark inside. By the time I reached the Olde Sweet Shoppe on the corner of the square I was downcast. The window displayed rows of glass jars, each full of sugary concoctions that held no appeal whatsoever for a cat in desperate need of a good meal.

By now the market traders had packed their vans and left, and the dark streets had begun to empty of pedestrians. I felt a growing sense of panic, wondering where I could go to find food. I ran across the square towards an entrance gate, through which I could see an imposing brick building set back amidst a well-kept garden. A smartly dressed couple hurried past me and made their way through the grounds towards the building's floodlit entrance. I followed them, mindful to keep a discreet distance, and as they pushed open the heavy wooden door, the delicious aroma of cooked food drifted down the path towards me. I climbed a grassy bank and nestled under the branches of a yew tree, from where I could see into the restaurant inside.

I was transfixed by the luxurious scene on the other side of the glass. Diners sat at linen-covered tables, their faces lit by the glow from flickering candles. Some of them wore coloured paper crowns, the kind I remembered Margery wearing as she ate Christmas lunch. They looked pink-cheeked and in high spirits, refilling their glasses with growing frequency as their crowns slipped forward over their eyes. The sound of their laughter pierced the stillness outside, and I watched in fascination as waiters glided between the tables, placing plates of food in front of them with great ceremony. Women in heavy jewellery pushed food demurely around their plates, flicking glossy hair over their shoulders with an air of nonchalance.

Could there be a potential owner for me among this restaurant's clientele? Surely some of them must be cat-lovers, I thought, but how was I to know which? I recalled the reaction of the woman I had followed at the farm shop: her face had shown undisguised revulsion when she had discovered me loitering near her car.

Studying the perfectly groomed women in the restaurant, I felt sure they too would not welcome any overture of friendliness from a cat that looked the way I did.

The screech of an owl in the treetops above me brought an end to my musings. I did not have time to allow myself to dwell on my hardships. I needed to find something to eat.

10

Dense shrubbery ran around the edge of the restaurant's grounds and it did not take me long to hunt a mouse. The rain had slowed to a light drizzle, and I allowed myself the luxury of a perfunctory wash under a rhododendron bush whilst waiting for my meal to settle. By the time I had finished, the clouds had cleared to leave a cold, starry night. The air temperature was dropping and the ground underneath my paws was beginning to harden. My next challenge was to find somewhere dry to spend the night.

Padding across the flowerbeds at the back of the restaurant, I noticed a short flight of stone steps leading to the street below. I crept silently down the steps, finding myself on a narrow, shop-lined road. A street light opposite illuminated the entrance to an alleyway between two shop fronts. Keen to get off the exposed pavement, I ran over and took a few tentative steps into the alley. It was enclosed by drystone walls, but up ahead I could see the backs of houses that bordered it on both sides.

As I inched along the path I scrutinized the windows of the houses that overlooked me. I felt a surge of optimism as I made out signs of human habitation within: pot plants on the windowsills, the flickering light from television sets, and dishes stacked messily next to sinks. Glimpsing the domestic clutter of strangers, I felt a wave of homesickness that made my throat tighten and eyes prickle. How I longed to be a part of someone's home once more, to feel the warm glow of security that comes from being in familiar surroundings, knowing that you are safe and loved.

I wanted to get closer to the houses, to peer through the windows and see the people who lived inside, but it felt as though the further I went along the alley, the more isolated I became. The alley was unlit and silent, apart from the clicking of my claws against the path. The hairs on my neck bristled as I thought I heard something move on the other side of the wall. I froze on the spot, my ears twisting to locate the source of the sound, but the alley was silent again. I took a deep breath, telling myself that what I had heard was an echo of my own footsteps. Trying not to panic, I picked up my pace to a trot, my eyes fixed on the alley's exit up ahead.

Suddenly there was movement on the wall above me. A security light on the back of one of the houses flashed on, and for a few seconds everything was lit up by a blinding white light. I backed against the wall and turned my head frantically from side to side, but I could see only the empty alley. The security light flicked off, everything went black and I held my breath as my eyes readjusted to the darkness.

My blood was thudding in my ears and I felt as though every hair on my body had stood on end. There was a scuffling noise on the wall, and I glanced up to see a shadowy shape leap down onto the path in front of me. I gasped, finding myself face-to-face with the orange eyes of a ginger tomcat. His spine was arched and his ears were pinned back against his head as he growled menacingly. Instinctively my body posture mirrored his. My back arched and I flattened my ears, letting out a low growl of warning. The ginger cat didn't move a muscle. His narrow eyes were still fixed on mine, daring me to make the first move. He was a large, intimidating creature, his physical strength evident in his muscular frame. The patchwork of scars on his ears left me in no doubt that he was an experienced fighter. I had my back to the wall, and to escape I would have to run past him, exposing my vulnerable rear to his attacks. He began to yowl again, as if challenging me to try.

Suddenly there was a scraping noise from above, as someone slid open a window in one of the houses. Startled, the tomcat spun round to look, and I seized my chance, bolting back down the alley in the direction of the restaurant steps. I heard scuffling behind me and knew that the tomcat was in pursuit. I sprinted towards the halo of lamplight that glowed at the end of the alley, but as I ran, my energy start to sap away. The exhaustion of my long walk in the rain was taking its toll and I could feel the strength draining from my muscles. I knew the tomcat was gaining ground and I braced myself for the inevitable attack.

It came in the form of a searing hot pain in one of my back legs. I instinctively kicked out at my attacker and he, having delivered his knockout blow, backed off. I turned and hissed at him, aware of the burning sensation that was spreading down my leg and making my paw feel as though it was on fire. A cruel smile spread across the tomcat's eyes as he looked at me.

'Sorry,' he said with a leer. 'This alley's taken.'

'You only needed to say,' I answered pitifully. He grinned as I limped towards the end of the alley.

Back out on the street, I felt light-headed, shaking with shock at what had just happened. I didn't know where to go, but I knew I had to get as far away from the alley as possible. Trying not to put any weight on my injured leg, I retraced the route I had taken earlier, limping across the restaurant grounds until I found myself back in the market square. The pain in my leg was becoming unbearable and I knew I urgently needed to find somewhere under cover to tend to the wound. I hobbled towards a large yellow skip by the side of the kerb on the corner of the square. The skip was overflowing with rubble and waste, and stacked up beside it were piles of wooden crates and pallets. There was a musty, dirty smell coming from the crates, but I didn't care. I forced myself through a gap between two pallets and burrowed forward until I reached the cold metal of the skip.

I slowly lowered myself to the ground and twisted round to examine my injured leg. The puncture wounds left by the tomcat's teeth were visible through my fur, and I could see that the flesh around them was swollen and tender. I licked the area as gently as I could, trying to minimize the pain that my rough tongue inflicted on the inflamed flesh. Once I was satisfied the wound was clean, I curled into a ball, hoping that sleep would provide some respite from my suffering. But when I closed my eyes I saw a muddled amalgamation of memories from the day: the red-faced diners in the restaurant, the ginger tom's leering eyes, the rain-soaked shoppers their faces hidden by umbrellas.

Desperate to put a stop to the endless loop of unsettling images, I forced myself to think of Margery. I tried to imagine her stroking and comforting me, telling me that it would all be better in the morning. But I couldn't summon up a clear picture of her face – it was as if she was out of focus somehow, her features vague and blurry. I didn't know if it was the effect of the bite or if I had simply forgotten what she looked like, but no matter how hard I tried, I couldn't hold her face in my mind. It was a bitter blow. I felt like I was losing Margery all over again, just at the moment when I needed her most.

11

Unable to sleep, I shivered next to the skip in a feverish state, convinced I could see the amber eyes of the alley-cat glaring at me through the pallets, or hear his menacing yowl somewhere in the square. It was impossible to find a comfortable position and I experienced a searing hot pain whenever I moved my leg. Time passed agonizingly slowly as I hovered on the edge of consciousness until my mind eventually succumbed to exhaustion and I dropped into a blissful blackness.

I was woken with a start by a chorus of human voices singing nearby. I lifted my head and listened, my ears twitching at the familiar-sounding music. Margery had loved to listen to music like this on her radio at Christmas, singing along happily while she prepared our Christmas dinner.

The throbbing in my leg snapped me out of my reverie. I winced as I stretched my leg out to examine it, but was glad to see that the swelling had gone down and the puncture marks had begun to scab over. I washed the wound, then slowly stood up, using my front legs to support my weight while I cautiously straightened my hind legs underneath me. I was wobbly, but apart from some soreness around the bite mark and a residual ache in the leg, I felt okay. I arched my back in a stretch, relieved to feel that my mind was at one with my body once more.

Crawling out of the pile of crates, I squinted in the winter sun. The town square was almost unrecognizable from the rain-soaked scene of the previous night. The shops were open and busy with customers. The yellow stone walls of the buildings on all sides glowed warmly against the blue sky, and their windows sparkled as they reflected the bright morning sunlight. The Christmas carollers who had woken me were standing in a semicircle in the middle of the square, wearing heavy coats zipped up to their chins. They all smiled as they sang, and one of them rattled a bucket full of loose change at passers-by.

Careful not to put any weight on my injured leg, I made my way gingerly around the square. The alley-cat's parting words – *This alley's taken* – were playing on my mind. Hobbling slowly along the pavement, I noticed for the first time that there were alleyways all around the square, their entrances so narrow and inconspicuous that I hadn't seen them the night before. Spotting the telltale gap between a sweet shop and the bakery, I tiptoed over and stood at the alley's entrance. I sniffed the stone, but could not detect any traces of feline scent. In the morning sunshine, with the occasional shopper passing through, the alley did not look terrifying. If it wasn't already taken by another cat, perhaps this was my chance to mark out a territory for myself.

I took a few steps along the alleyway and made use of a litter bin to jump up onto the top of the wall that ran alongside the path. My hackles rose instinctively when I saw the unmistakeable shape of a cat up ahead, basking in the sunshine on the flat roof of a shed. My tail flicked from side to side as I considered what to do next. I tiptoed closer. The cat was fast asleep, a neat crescent of tortoiseshell fur, with her tail tucked snugly around her body. Her eyes were shut tight and she had tilted her face up towards the sun, with her mouth curled into a smile. I stood on the wall, watching her fur rise and fall with her breath, envying her ability to feel relaxed enough to sleep out in the open.

The sound of dogs barking in the square brought her nap to an abrupt end. She jerked her head upright, ears flicking in response to the noise. Her eyes had opened, but the inner eyelids were still visible as she made the sudden shift from sleep to consciousness. She looked around and, noticing me on the wall, jumped to her feet and began to growl.

'Who are you? What do you want?' she hissed.

'I'm Molly. Sorry – I didn't mean to scare you.' I replied in the calmest voice I could muster, though I was beginning to shake with fear.

The cat glared at me. She looked young, but there was no mistaking her threatening demeanour.

'I'm new to the town,' I continued, my tone placatory. 'I'm just looking around. Getting to know the place.'

She eyed me suspiciously and I blinked slowly, then averted my gaze, the universal feline indicator of non-aggression.

'You're new round here?' she repeated.

I nodded. 'I've been walking for weeks, got here last night. I'm looking for somewhere to live, but I was attacked in an alley last night.'

I saw her eyes flash – I wasn't sure whether with anger or concern.

'You can't just come and go as you please, you know. There are rules.' She frowned as she looked me up and down. I sensed her confusion, and that she was unsure whether to regard me as a threat or take pity on me.

'So is this . . . your alley?' I enquired, glancing at her

face, in the hope that she might say more to enlighten me.

'Yes.' Her eyes held mine for a moment, then she went on, 'They're all taken. The alley-cats have them marked out. Where did you say you were attacked?'

I described the alley behind the restaurant, and the ginger tom with amber eyes. She winced.

'Hmm. I know the one you mean. Bad move. Really bad.' She registered my look of dismay. 'It's probably best if you avoid the alleys, at least until you've settled in a bit,' she explained in a conciliatory tone.

My head was spinning. It was starting to dawn on me that the town's alleyways were a network of feline territories and that, in my naivety, I had stumbled into the domain of a notorious fighter. I didn't know whether to feel sorry for my bad luck or to berate my ignorance for not acting with more caution.

'I'm hoping to find an owner, really. Someone who loves cats. A home.' I could feel moisture welling up in my eyes.

The tortoiseshell cat looked at me pityingly. 'You'll have a job round here. The people in this town are all about their dogs, in case you haven't noticed. Cats don't get a look-in,' she said ruefully.

As if on cue, a woman walking a dog entered the alley. The dog growled and lunged forwards, straining against his collar to reach us. The tortoiseshell cat jumped to her feet, hackles raised, and hissed at the dog as he passed in front of us.

'Look, I'm sorry. Why don't you try the churchyard? You should at least find shelter there. But you've got to leave now – I shouldn't even be talking to you.'

She leapt from the shed roof up into the branches of a tree while I stayed on the shed roof, eyeballing the dog as he was dragged away down the alley. When he had gone I looked up into the tree, but the tortoiseshell cat had disappeared.

Feeling disconsolate, I made my way across the square in the direction of the church spire. I entered the churchyard through a wooden gate, savouring the peaceful atmosphere, which was in stark contrast to the bustle of the square. A pigeon cooed from the church roof as I settled down behind a row of headstones for a wash. I wasn't sure how I felt about the tortoiseshell cat's revelations. To be told that the alleyways were, in effect, no-go areas for me was disheartening; but, I reminded myself, it wasn't an alley I wanted, it was a home, and an owner. More worrying was her dismissal of my chances of finding someone to take me in. If she was right, and people in Stourton cared only for dogs, I would have made a grave error in coming to this town at all.

My wash complete, I pushed through a row of conifers that bordered the churchyard and found myself in a short parade of shops along a cobbled street. There was a café at the far end of the row, with a rusty metal table and chairs standing outside its door. I padded along the cobbles to get a better look at the café. Paint was peeling from the frames of its curved bay window, and the solitary string of fairy lights draped inside did not do much to improve the café's shabby appearance. The sign above the door read 'Church Café' and I was relieved to see a sticker in the window saying 'Sorry: no dogs'. My impression of a rather down-at-heel establishment was confirmed when I peered through the glass door and saw a few rickety tables in front of an ugly serving counter.

I made my way round to the side of the café, and my heart sank to see that an alleyway ran behind it. The rear of the café and its adjoining shops presented a mismatched vista of windows, fire escapes and air vents. A large, square dustbin was pushed against the back wall of the café, only a few feet away from where I was standing. Its lid was damaged at one corner, revealing the polythene bags full of food waste underneath. I sniffed the air, detecting the unmistakeable aroma of tuna mayonnaise, and my stomach rumbled in response. Uncertain what to do, I twitched my tail. The dustbin was only a few paces away, but dare I risk a repeat of last night's ambush by whichever cat 'owned' this alley? Still weakened from yesterday's encounter, I would be in no state to defend myself.

A gust of wind wafted the scent of tuna in my direction and my mind was made up. Nancy had helped me to perfect my scavenging technique, so I knew it wouldn't take long to do what was needed. I ran over to the bin and dropped to my haunches, crouching low to the ground. I felt my leg spasm in pain as I sprang upwards, but I made a perfect landing on top of the lid, feeling the bin's contents give slightly under my weight. I balanced on the edge of the dustbin and batted at one of the bags until my claws caught and I could rip it open. There was a satisfying splattering sound as a mound of sandwich filling dropped onto the ground. I hopped down and greedily set about eating the pile of tuna mayonnaise. After my recent diet of mice and shrews, it tasted delicious. Savouring the feeling of having a full belly, I turned to leave the alley, and almost jumped out of my skin at finding myself face-to-face with a black-and-white tomcat.

12

The tomcat stood at the alley's entrance, frozen in mid-step with one paw hovering above the ground. His expression suggested surprise rather than hostility but, with last night's trauma still fresh in my mind, I immediately braced myself for a fight. Arching my back and fluffing out my tail, I growled deeply and hissed, warning him to back off. The tomcat tilted his head to one side, observing my display of aggression with curiosity.

'Good morning,' he said, his green eyes looking at me calmly. 'Have you finished?' He glanced over my shoulder at the dustbin. His unexpected politeness disarmed me and, unsure whether I could trust him, I maintained my defensive pose and let out another growl. A smile flickered across his eyes and he sat down on the path, casually lifting a paw to wash his face, as if to suggest that he was happy to wait. I sized him up while he groomed himself, seemingly oblivious to my presence.

His sleek fur was black all over, but for a patch of white on his chest and the long white whiskers which framed his square face. He was long-legged and rangy, clearly in his physical prime. As he continued to ignore me, my feeling of alarm began to turn to embarrassment – my terrified response was beginning to seem like something of an overreaction. I self-consciously relaxed my back and lowered my hackles, but in spite of my efforts to control it, my tail remained in its voluminously fluffy state. I saw the tomcat glance at it as he washed, and I felt mortified, as if it somehow gave away my inexperience and vulnerability. He seemed to sense my awkwardness and averted his eyes, turning away to lick his back while I tried to regain my composure. It was only when he stopped washing and looked at me expectantly that I realized that he had asked me a question and was still waiting for a reply.

'Yes, I'm finished,' I stuttered. 'I hope I didn't eat your . . .' I tailed off apologetically, painfully aware of the incriminating smell of tuna that was emanating from my whiskers.

"S'all right,' the cat replied, 'plenty more where that came from.'

He stood up and walked towards me. I felt my fur

bristle in alarm, but he maintained a respectful distance as he walked around me, on his way to the dustbin. While he began to root around in the bin's contents, I retreated further down the alley to observe him from behind a pile of cardboard boxes. He was in good condition, not scarred and battle-torn like the ginger cat, and seemed too friendly to be an alley-cat. But if he was a pet with a home, what was he doing scavenging for food in a dustbin?

When he had finished eating, he wiped his whiskers with his paw, before sloping off in the direction of the churchyard. As he passed my hiding place he looked towards me and nodded once, as if to let me know that he had known I was there all along. He didn't break his stride, however, and continued to the end of the alley before disappearing into darkness beneath the conifers.

For a few moments I stared down the empty alley, my heart sinking as I realized that, once again, I had misjudged the situation and made a fool of myself. The tomcat's behaviour seemed to throw all of my newly acquired assumptions about alley-cats into disarray. My initial relief that our encounter had passed without confrontation soon gave way to frustration that, in my panic, I had forgone the opportunity to ask his advice. Part of me wanted to run after him – to tell him how I had ended up here, and to ask him what I should do next. But the events of the previous twenty-four hours had taught me to exercise caution. The tomcat might have allowed me to eat from a bin in his alley, but I didn't want to push my luck by pestering him for help.

Drowsiness was beginning to spread over me, as the soporific effect of my meal took hold. The cardboard boxes provided surprisingly effective insulation against the draughts that whipped down through the alley, and for the first time since arriving in Stourton I felt a sense of well-being. Listening to the magpies chattering in the nearby churchyard, I curled up and fell into a deep, restorative sleep.

I was awoken by the sound of the church bells, and I lifted my head to listen as they chimed six times. Night had fallen and I could make out the muffled sound of the church organ drifting through the air. My fur prickled as I heard the rattling of a key in the back door of the café. I peered round the edge of my cardboard shelter and watched as a woman stepped outside, clutching a black polythene bag. From my hiding place I could not see her face, only that she had shoulder-length blonde hair and was wearing a light cotton jumper and jeans. She lifted the lid of the dustbin and tossed the bag inside, trying in vain to press the lid shut on top of its overflowing contents. She shivered in the cold, before rushing back inside and slamming the door shut behind her.

The aroma of fresh food drifted towards me and

my mouth began to water. Scanning the alley to make sure I was alone, I ran over to the bin and jumped onto the lid. I ripped the bag open and was delighted to see copious amounts of smoked-salmon and chicken mayonnaise drop onto the path below. Purring with pleasure, I jumped down and feasted quickly on the sandwich fillings, alert for the tomcat's return. As soon as I had finished, I ran back over to the cardboard boxes, curious to know whether the tomcat would reappear for his evening meal.

Sure enough, a little later I heard rustling in the conifers, and saw his silhouette slink silently in front of my hiding place. This time he seemed genuinely oblivious to my presence as he ate. Observing him through a gap between two cardboard boxes, I was struck by how at ease he looked in the alley. I was convinced now that he was the alley's resident cat, but I was surprised that, rather than feeling afraid of him, I found his presence reassuring.

I was woken during the night by ear-splitting yowling, the unmistakeable preamble to a cat-fight. For a horrible moment I wondered if my hiding place had been discovered by the ginger cat and I was under attack. I remained silent and motionless, relying on my ears to discern what was happening. There were two cats in the alley, mere inches from my shelter, growling and hissing in a noisy stand-off. My heart raced. One of them was surely the black-and-white tom, but who was his adversary?

I remained petrified inside my box, feeling at once terrified and guilty that I was not doing anything to help. There was a momentary silence followed by a scuffle. The yowling stopped and I could hear bodies writhing on the path, the eerie quiet punctuated by yelps of protest. Eventually I heard a hiss as a cat ran out of the alley, and then there was silence once more. My curiosity to know who had won was more than I could bear, and I peeked out into the alley. The tomcat was sitting at the entrance, his inky profile silhouetted against the glow of the street light beyond. There was no sign of his opponent, and he was calmly smoothing his fur with his tongue. I crawled back into my cardboard shelter, more certain than ever that the alley was his territory.

The following morning he was sitting on top of the dustbin when I emerged from my box, sleepy but hungry.

'Oh, hello,' I said nervously, determined to appear more coherent than I had on our first meeting.

'Good morning. Did you sleep well?'

'Yes, thank you. And are you . . . okay?' I added, thinking of the fight I had heard during the night.

'Never been better,' he answered, a smile in his eyes.

There was no evidence on his body that he had been fighting and he seemed in remarkably good spirits after his ordeal. I felt slightly in awe that he had managed to come unscathed out of such a nasty-sounding battle, and I even wondered whether I had dreamt the whole thing. He stood up and stretched, before jumping down onto the path.

'There's some left,' he said, gesturing with his head towards the rubbish bags protruding from under the lid. 'Won't be any new stuff till this evening, so make the most of it.' As he strode purposefully past me on his way to the churchyard, I noticed how the muscles around his shoulders rippled under his fur.

'Oh, thanks,' I replied meekly.

I waited until he had vanished into the conifers, before jumping onto the bin. Through the gap in the lid I could see a small amount of leftover sandwich fillings inside a ripped bag. A perfect portion-size for a cat, in fact. For a moment I wondered if the tomcat had purposely saved some for me, rather than eaten it all himself, but I quickly dismissed the thought from my mind. He was an alley-cat, after all. Why would he do such a thing?

13

The alley was rarely used by passers-by, due to it being blocked at one end by the churchyard conifers. I liked its peaceful, enclosed atmosphere; it felt safe, far removed from the dangers of the busy town beyond. I made a shelter underneath the spiral steps of a fire escape at the back of a shop, to which I returned every night, curling up to sleep on a flattened piece of cardboard behind a stack of rusty paint tins.

It didn't take me long to adjust to the rhythm of life in the alley. I soon learnt that six o'clock was the café's closing time, and that the day's food waste would be put out shortly afterwards. The church bells' sonorous clanging became my cue to return, in hungry anticipation of an evening meal of leftover sandwich fillings. I rarely saw the tomcat during the day – he roamed much further afield than I did – but sometimes our paths crossed as we both trotted hungrily towards the dustbin in the evening. He was always courteous, chivalrously allowing me to eat before he did, but I nevertheless remained slightly in awe of him. I sensed his territorial vigilance and, having overheard the fight on my first night, knew that he was capable of defending himself fiercely. I did not want to do anything that might make him regret his tolerance towards me.

A couple of weeks after my arrival I noticed that the colourful lights had disappeared from the shop-front windows along the parade. The cobbled street seemed in a permanent half-light under low-slung winter cloud and had a melancholy feeling, stripped of the cheerful presence of Christmas decorations. The street seemed emptier of people too, as if the town's residents had gone into hibernation after the exuberance of the festive period.

One morning I woke to discover the first snowfall of winter had transformed the alley overnight and the path had disappeared under a thick blanket of white. I had loved to watch snow falling when I was a house-cat. I would sit on Margery's patio and peer up as the fluffy flakes floated down, resting tantalizingly on my nose and whiskers before melting into my fur. I had found snow fascinating back then, safe in the knowledge that I was never more than a few feet from the comfort of Margery's gas fire.

In the alley, however, the snow posed serious difficulties for me. It coated the iron steps of the fire escape where, thawed by the warmth of the building behind, icy droplets dripped onto me as I tried to sleep. As if to compensate for the bitter environment, my fur grew denser than I had ever known it before, a thick pelt designed to hold in as much warmth as possible. But, even with the extra insulation, I felt permanently chilled. There was nowhere I could go to escape the cold, and my only option was to retreat to my shelter and tend to my footpads, which were chapped and cracked from the icy ground. I passed many hours curled in a tight ball trying to keep warm, praying for sleep to bring me a few hours' respite.

If I craned my neck, I could see the café door through a gap between the paint tins. I studied the woman from the café closely whenever she emerged from inside. She was younger than Margery – I guessed in her late forties – with kind blue eyes that often had a doleful look. Sometimes she would stand at the foot of the metal stairs, inches away from my bed, chatting with the woman who ran the hardware shop which adjoined the café.

Silent and unobserved, I listened to their conversations. I learnt that her name was Debbie, that she had recently moved to Stourton with her daughter, Sophie, and that they lived in the flat above the café. Weak from the winter cold, I found comfort in the softness of her voice, closing my eyes and allowing my mind to wander as she talked. I daydreamed about life inside the flat above the café, imagining a cosy room with an open fire where I could lie, my belly exposed to the flames, before retreating to a cool sofa when the heat became too much. I pictured Debbie curled up on the sofa next to me, stroking me gently while she read a book, both of us enjoying the bliss of each other's company.

In the past I wouldn't have thought twice about throwing myself on Debbie's mercy, hoping that she would take pity on me and offer me a home. But I knew how much was at stake: if Debbie knew there were stray cats in the alley, she might go to more effort to secure the dustbin and our food supply could be cut off. The tomcat always avoided being seen by Debbie and I deferred to his experience, subduing my natural inclination towards sociability and staying hidden from sight.

In the end, Debbie discovered my existence by accident. The snow had finally begun to thaw and the icy water dripped relentlessly onto my bed from above, driving me out of the fire escape and into the alley. It was late morning, a time when I knew Debbie would be busy at the front of the café. The winter sun was low, but there was the faintest hint of warmth in its pale rays, so I sat down next to the dustbin, savouring the feeling of fresh air in my whiskers. I began to wash, tilting my body backwards to lift my hind leg behind my ear. Just at that moment the café door opened. I turned to see Debbie step out of the doorway, clutching a bag of rubbish. She looked straight at me and I froze, hoping that if I stayed completely still she might not notice me.

'Oh, hello, puss.' She sounded surprised, but I detected a smile in her voice. I stood up to move away from the bin, not wanting her to think I was scavenging, but was startled to feel her hand on my back, stroking my spine down to the base of my tail. I reflexively lifted my back in response to her touch, realizing with a pang how long it had been since I had last been stroked, and how much I had missed it. I twisted my head to look at her and she held her fingers out to me and, as I sniffed her skin, she tickled me under the chin. The automatic way in which she had responded to me seemed to confirm my deepest hope, that this was a woman who knew how to love a cat.

'You're a pretty thing, aren't you?' she said, smiling, and I chirruped in agreement. I was hoping to engage her in a longer exchange, but a voice from inside the café shouted, 'Mum, where are you? I can't find my homework!' Debbie sighed, tossed the bag of rubbish into the bin and then was gone, pulling the café door shut behind her. I stared at the door for several minutes afterwards, hoping she might come out again, but to no avail. Eventually I resumed my wash, my head suddenly flooded with bittersweet memories of how it felt to bask in the affection of a loving owner.

Encouraged by Debbie's friendliness, I became braver about making my presence known in the alley. Rather than hiding out of sight when she was around, I took to waiting by the bin at the café's closing time, in full view of the door. When I heard the key rattling in the lock I would trot over and rub my head against the doorframe in expectation. 'Good evening, puss. How are you today?' Debbie would say, her blue eyes twinkling as she carried the bags over my head to the bin. I would stick close to her ankles, purring, my tail erect.

A few days later, when Debbie unlocked door one evening, she was holding a dish in her hand. I could smell smoked salmon and tuna mayonnaise and I instinctively reared up onto my hind legs to get closer to the bowl. She placed it on the doorstep in front of me, scratching the base of my tail playfully. 'There you go, puss. Now leave the bags alone, okay?' she laughed, as I greedily tucked into the bowl's contents.

She went back inside and I carried on eating, savouring the way the leftovers tasted so much better from a bowl than from the tarmac. Sensing that I was being watched, I glanced over my shoulder, spotting the dark shape of the black-and-white tom in the shadow of the dustbin. I swallowed my mouthful and licked my lips, before padding towards him. 'I'm done. There's plenty left, if you'd like it,' I said with a look of encouragement. The tomcat's eyes flashed uncertainly towards the café door. 'She's friendly, you know,' I reassured him. 'You should get to know her. She's a nice lady.'

The tomcat inclined his head. 'I'm not really a "nice lady" kind of cat,' he replied. 'Never have been.'

His comment perplexed me. I tried to imagine *not* being a 'nice lady' kind of cat. To me, that was like saying I was not a 'tuna mayonnaise' kind of cat. Granted, I had learnt that I could survive without nice ladies or tuna mayonnaise, but that was not to say I would ever choose to. The tomcat paced gingerly towards the bowl, where he ate quickly, glancing at the café door nervously in between mouthfuls.

It was obvious that being so close to the café made him anxious, but I felt a glow of satisfaction that, by eating the food she had put out, he had acknowledged that my friendship with Debbie could benefit us both. The tomcat seemed so self-assured in every other respect, but when it came to dealing with people I realized he was distinctly nervous. This was the one area in which I was the more experienced, the more worldly, of the two of us. In befriending Debbie, I had done something he had been too frightened to do himself and, for the first time since I had arrived in the alley, I felt like his equal.

Later that night, I was settling down under the fire escape when I heard claws clicking along the path. My chin was resting on my paws, but my ears were alert, monitoring the progress of the footsteps as they approached. I held my breath as the clicking came to a halt outside my shelter. A long shadow appeared on the wall behind me. 'Oh, it's you,' I said, sighing with relief as the familiar silhouette of the tomcat appeared beside the paint tins.

14

Before I had set off for Stourton, Nancy had given me some advice about how to attract a new owner. She said that people like to pursue a cat, to earn her affections, rather than feel the cat is pursuing them. 'Don't seem desperate,' she had urged. 'It puts people off.' I had been sceptical at the time: the notion of acting aloofly with a potential owner struck me as illogical. 'Well, look, it worked for me, six times over!' she had replied, and I couldn't argue with her success rate. Fearful of what was at stake if I came on too strong with Debbie, I knew that Nancy would tell me to bide my time. So that was what I did, waiting for Debbie to realize that she wanted me to be part of her life.

While I perfected my friendly-but-not-needy de-meanour, I continued to gather intelligence about Debbie from my shelter under the fire escape. I learnt from eavesdropping on her conversations that she and

Sophie had moved to Stourton from Oxford a few months previously, following Debbie's divorce from Sophie's dad. Sophie was in the middle of preparing for her GCSEs, and had found the move difficult. A look of sadness always appeared on Debbie's face when Jo from the hardware shop asked after Sophie. Her brow would knit with anxiety as she explained that Sophie was 'still finding her feet' or 'struggling to settle in'.

Sophie appeared in the alleyway every day after school, a tatty rucksack slung over her shoulder and white headphones attached to her ears. Sometimes she would stand on the path, intently tapping at her mobile phone before entering the café and slamming the door shut behind her. Her arrival in the upstairs flat would usually be heralded by a blast of loud music from one of the attic windows.

From time to time I heard Debbie and Sophie arguing in the evenings. Their words were muffled by the thick stone walls of the flat, but my ears pricked up as I recognized the unmistakeable tone of conflict. Sophie's voice would always be the first I heard, sharp and accusatory, followed by placatory-sounding noises from Debbie. Gradually their voices would rise in pitch and volume until they were both shouting. The rows always ended the same way, with Sophie storm-ing out into the alley, plugging in her headphones and stalking off.

On one occasion, Sophie slammed the café door shut behind her with such ferocity that the birds on the roof were sent flapping upwards in alarm. Debbie, who was wearing her dressing-gown and slippers, followed her daughter out into the alley, pleading with her to come back inside, but to no avail. Sophie had disappeared round the corner, leaving Debbie standing alone in the cold night air. Debbie turned to head back inside, and my heart welled with pity at the desolate look on her face. I crept out from under the fire escape and trotted over to her, mewing cheerfully. She smiled and bent down to stroke me. 'I'm not that bad, am I, puss?' she asked sadly. I wrapped myself around her legs and purred until I saw a faint smile appear around her lips. I stayed close to her ankles as she walked to the door but when, as usual, she stopped me at the threshold, I retreated obediently to my shelter.

Sometimes, after darkness had fallen, I would jump onto the dustbin and watch Debbie through the window as she cleared up at the end of the day. The café kitchen was lit up by strips of harsh yellow lights, which gleamed brilliantly on the stainless-steel surfaces. Unaware that I was watching her, Debbie would move around the kitchen placing plastic containers in the fridge, wiping down worktops and washing up in the sink. She usually sang to herself as she worked, but occasionally her voice would tail off and she would stare out of the window, looking preoccupied and thoughtful.

The first time it happened I thought she was staring at me, and my heart lurched in hope that she had noticed me and might be about to invite me in. But I quickly realized I was invisible to her in the dark alley, and that all she could see in the window was the reflection of the brightly lit kitchen around her. Rather than looking at me, she was simply gazing into space, lost in thought. It reminded me a little of how Margery had acted in the early days of her illness, becoming distracted in the middle of a domestic chore, her mind wandering away to some place where I couldn't follow her. I studied Debbie's face, looking for clues as to what might be going on in her mind, fearing that this momentary distraction would be followed by the confusion and distress that I had seen so often in Margery. But these episodes only ever lasted for a few seconds, after which Debbie would give her head a quick shake and carry on with her task, and I would breathe a sigh of relief.

It was easy to lose track of time as I gazed at Debbie through the window, and I maintained my surveillance from the dustbin until she had turned off the lights and gone upstairs. Sometimes, as I made my way back to the fire escape, I would notice the green eyes of the tomcat fixed on me as he lurked in the shadows. The sight of him always made me jump, and I would wonder how long he had been there, watching me as I had been watching Debbie, and what thoughts lay behind his intense stare.

The epiphany that I had been waiting for finally happened on a grey, wet evening at the end of January. It was raining steadily but, rather than seeking shelter from the rain, I sat on the doorstep, listening to the gurgling drainpipe as I waited for six o'clock. Unpleasant as it was, getting drenched was part of my plan. I had followed Nancy's advice by not being too needy, but now I decided Debbie would benefit from a less subtle approach. It was a gamble, but for my plan to work I needed to look a sorry sight when she opened the door and found me. As the church bells chimed six, I heard Debbie unlock the door. 'Oh dear, puss, look at the state of you,' she said pityingly, exactly as I had hoped she would.

I gazed at her and mouthed a silent meow. She frowned, bending down to wipe some of the rainwater off my coat, and I rubbed my face against her hand gratefully. She looked concerned as she crouched down to place the food bowl in front of me. I resisted the urge to bury my face in the bowl, knowing that if I did, she would stand up and turn to go inside. Instead I ignored the food and held her gaze. It was raining hard and before long she was almost as sodden as I was. I mouthed another plea at her, following it up with a rub of my head against her knees.

She closed her eyes and sighed deeply, before standing up. With one hand on the door handle, she dropped her head as if in submission. 'I suppose you might as well come in, puss,' she said, a smile of surrender on her face. She pushed open the café door and, without so much as a backward glance, I trotted inside.

15

Debbie placed the bowl in front of me on the kitchen floor, so I ate a few mouthfuls out of courtesy, although my appetite had vanished in my excitement at being allowed in. When I felt I had eaten enough not to appear ungrateful, I padded through to the front of the café while Debbie finished her chores in the kitchen.

The café was lit only by the glow of the street lights outside, but even in the dark I knew that my initial impression of a rundown establishment had been well founded. Much of the floor area was taken up with an ugly glass-and-metal serving counter, its plastic shelves yellowing with age. I tiptoed between wobbly aluminium tables and sniffed at the musty linoleum underfoot. There was a black stove in the stone fireplace, but it was cold to the touch and, judging by the dust that coated it, looked like it had not been used for a long time.

It felt strange to be inside again after so long out-doors. The atmosphere seemed enclosed, the background soundtrack of birds in distant treetops replaced by the electrical hum of kitchen appliances. I turned and walked towards the curved bay window at the front of the café, jumping onto the windowsill to look out through the square panes of glass. The street outside was deserted, and raindrops bounced silently on the wet cobbles.

Debbie switched off the kitchen lights and walked through to the café. I hopped down from the window and approached her with my tail up in greeting. She sat down at a little table and held a hand out towards me, smiling. I trotted over and leapt up onto her lap, purring my gratitude that she had finally taken me in. The sound of sniffing made me look up, and I was dis-mayed to see that tears were sliding down Debbie's cheeks as she stroked me. I blinked slowly at her, trying to communicate that she might feel better if she talked to me. She sighed and rubbed me behind the ears.

'You know, puss, you're the first one to show me any affection in a long time,' she whispered. I licked her hand to reassure her that, if it was my affection she wanted, she had come to the right cat. She nuzzled her face against the back of my head while I kneaded her lap with my paws and we remained that way, sitting in the dark, silent café until eventually I dozed off. I was only vaguely aware of Debbie standing up underneath me, then carefully placing me back on the chair while I remained curled in a ball. I rearranged myself on the seat, which was still warm from her body. She whispered, 'Night-night, puss', before climbing the flight of stairs that led from the café to the flat above.

The next thing I knew, sunlight was streaming through the bay window and I could hear footsteps and voices through the ceiling. Startled momentarily to find that I was not under the fire escape in the alley, I sat up and looked around me. The drab greyness of the floor and dirty walls was even more apparent in the bright morning light. The woodwork, which had once been white, was yellow and peeling in places, and the metal tables were scratched. I heard a footfall and voices on the stairs.

Sophie was the first to appear in the café, glowering suspiciously at me. 'How do you know it hasn't got fleas, or worse?' she scowled.

'I'm sure she's perfectly healthy,' Debbie reassured her daughter from the stairwell. 'I just need you to keep an eye on the café for a couple of hours.'

'Well, she looks dirty to me,' Sophie replied in a surly tone, not taking her eyes off me.

I observed Sophie quizzically. She was a little taller

than Debbie and her long blonde hair was streaked with pink. It was a Saturday, and she was wearing a floral summer dress – somewhat incongruously, given the weather outside – over thick black tights and clumpy boots. I had seen her in the alley on many occasions, but never at such close quarters. She was a pretty girl, but her attractiveness was somwhat tempered by a permanent frown. Her blue eyes reminded me of Debbie's, but rather than kindness, they conveyed irritation and hostility. I was in no doubt that she was going to prove more of a challenge to win over than her mother.

A couple of moments later Debbie appeared behind Sophie at the foot of the stairs. Her face was obscured behind a large plastic box, which I immediately recognized as a cat carrier. My reflexes kicked in and I leapt from the chair with such force that it almost toppled over behind me. Sophie shrieked as I shot past her. Desperate to find somewhere to hide, I squeezed under the metal serving counter, pressed between its base and the dusty floor. The appearance of the cat carrier could mean only one thing: I was to be taken away, just as I had been from Margery. I cursed myself for being so naive.

I heard Debbie groan. She placed the carrier on a table, then knelt down next to my hiding place. One side of her face appeared, sideways, in the gap between the floor and the edge of the counter. 'It's all right, puss, please don't be scared,' she pleaded. I remained stony-faced.

'What if it bites you and gives you rabies?' Sophie asked scathingly.

Debbie's right cheek was pressed against the floor, and I saw her eye roll. 'Of course she hasn't got rabies, Sophie, don't be ridiculous. This is the Cotswolds.' She stretched her arm out awkwardly, wiggling her fingers at me in an effort to coax me towards her. 'Come on, puss, please come out,' she implored, but I stayed put. I knew that, if called upon, I could maintain my position much longer than she could, with her bottom in the air and her face wedged under the counter.

'I guess you won't be needing me to watch the café after all,' Sophie sneered. 'Doesn't look like you're going anywhere this morning.'

I heard her heavy boots stomp upstairs to the flat.

Debbie sighed and looked me in the eye. 'Please, puss. I just want to take you to the vet to get you checked over. I'm not going to hurt you, I promise.' I stared back impassively. She sighed and, with a few noises of discomfort, got to her feet. Dropping onto a nearby chair, she stretched out her legs and began to rub her knees.

Relieved to have some privacy, I took a moment to consider my options. I could make a dash for freedom as soon as the café door was opened, but where would I go? Would I have to start all over again – find a different alleyway, or another potential owner to charm? Or could I trust that what Debbie had said was true, that she was not planning to have me rehomed, but was simply taking me to the vet? Margery had done the same on a regular basis. It had never been the highlight of my year, involving needles being stuck between my shoulder blades and fingers prising my mouth open. But it was an ordeal to which I had become accustomed, and I appreciated that Margery did it with my best interests at heart.

I squirmed forward on my belly to the front edge of the counter. Debbie was still massaging her knees, gazing idly out of the bay window. I took a deep breath and sidled out from my hiding place. The cramped space had left my joints stiff, so I stretched out from nose to tail on the café floor, before padding over to Debbie and patting her shin with my paw.

'Oh!' she exclaimed, shocked to see that I had come out of my own accord. 'Oh, puss, look at the state of you!' she added, wiping the cobwebs and dust from my fur. 'Okay, puss, shall we get you to the vet?' she asked, looking me calmly in the eyes. I blinked at her.

Debbie called Sophie back downstairs, then lifted me gently into the carrier and walked me to her car. Talking to me in a low, soothing voice, she placed me on the passenger seat, before starting the engine. Being inside her car brought back memories of driving to Rob's house, and I was unable to stop myself from yowling in distress. Debbie responded to each yowl patiently. 'There, there, it'll be all right, puss.'

At the vets, Debbie explained that she had found me in the alleyway and wanted to keep me. The vet checked me over and pronounced me 'in remarkably good health for a stray'. She then ran a device that looked like a television remote control across my body to scan for a microchip. When the device started bleeping, Debbie's face fell. She shot a questioning look at the vet, who began to tap at her computer keyboard. 'According to the chip, her name's Molly,' she said.

'Oh, what a lovely name,' Debbie replied, a smile lighting up her eyes. 'I suppose she must be lost. Her owner's probably looking for her,' she continued. The smile had faded and she looked as if she was about to burst into tears.

'Let's call the number and find out, shall we?' the vet asked gently, and Debbie nodded.

The vet left the room and we waited, Debbie drumming her fingers on the black examination table while I tried to ignore the unpleasant smell of disinfectant. I wanted to reassure Debbie that I knew Margery wouldn't be able to look for me, and I very much doubted that Rob would have made any effort to. But we were both at the mercy of the vet and her phone call. There was nothing we could do except wait.

After what felt like an eternity, the vet came back into the room. 'The number's no longer in use, and without a current contact, there's not much we can do.' A grin began to spread across Debbie's face. 'Molly is officially a stray, and yours to rehome if you want to.' I'd never felt so happy to hear myself described as a stray, and there was no mistaking Debbie's elation as she burst into tears of relief and hugged me. I was given an injection before being returned to the cat carrier where I waited patiently while the vet typed Debbie's details into her computer. Once the registration process was complete, Debbie thanked the vet, picked up the handful of leaflets she had been given, and we were free to go.

'What do you think about that, Molly – you're officially my cat!' Debbie said cheerily as she placed me on the passenger seat of her car.

There was not much I could do to communicate my delight through the plastic of the carrier, but the happiness that rushed through my body made me feel like I was floating. I was so ecstatic that I didn't even mind when Debbie cranked up the volume on the car radio and sang along loudly for the entire duration of the journey home.

16

'Guess what, Soph. We have a new member of the family!'

Debbie swung the café door open triumphantly, brandishing the cat carrier in front of her. Sophie was sitting on a stool behind the serving counter, frowning as she swiped her thumb across her phone. A slight rolling of her eyes was the only indication that she had heard Debbie's words. Her apathy did nothing to dent my euphoria, however, as Debbie released me from the carrier into the empty café.

She gave me a quick rub behind the ears, before pulling an apron over her head and disappearing into the kitchen. Without acknowledging either of us, Sophie wordlessly grabbed her coat and vanished out onto the street. Realizing that I was free to explore, I headed upstairs, keen to see Debbie's home, and the rooms I had fantasized about for so long.

The flat was low-ceilinged and felt rather cramped, as if more rooms had been fitted inside than there was space to accommodate. A narrow hallway opened into a tiny kitchen and bathroom on one side, and a square room that overlooked the alley on the other. The room was fairly large, but was dominated by the dining table and chairs immediately in front of the door, and by a deep three-seater sofa along the wall. A modest television set stood in the alcove next to the open fireplace, which, I was disappointed to note, showed no signs of recent use. There was yellowing woodchip paper on the walls and a threadbare carpet underfoot, but Debbie had gone to great lengths to make it homely, with flowers on the dining table, soft rugs placed over the carpet and colourful pictures on the walls.

A short flight of stairs led from the hallway to Debbie and Sophie's compact bedrooms, tucked under the building's eaves. I poked my head around the door on my right, peering into what I deduced must be Sophie's room. I picked a fastidious route between the dirty clothes, balled-up tissues and damp towels that littered the floor. As I brushed past a chair I dislodged a messy heap of clothes, which had been thrown onto the seat-back. The pile toppled over, startling me as they hit the floor behind me. I dashed out of the room, hoping that, given the state of the rest of the bedroom, Sophie wouldn't notice the additional mess.

Debbie's room was no larger than Sophie's, but was much more welcoming. The bed was covered by a pretty patchwork quilt in shades of blue and silver. I padded across the floor to the dressing table, on which bottles and jars stood in neat rows. A heart-shaped wreath of dried lavender hung from the window above. I breathed deeply, detecting the faintest trace of a scent that would forever make me think of Margery.

Heading back down to the living room, I heard the radiators tick unevenly as the central heating slowed, and I took a moment to savour the fact that, since entering the café the previous day, I had not once felt cold. In the living room I jumped onto the sofa and washed thoroughly, in preparation for a nap, which I knew would be more comfortable than any I had had for months.

Over the next few days I began to settle in, and the flat and café gradually started to feel like home. Sophie was the only obstacle to my complete assimilation to life in the flat. She had been unimpressed by my arrival and remained stubbornly impervious to my attempts to charm her. She rarely noticed my existence and, if she did, her attitude was invariably hostile.

One afternoon, during my first week in the flat, I was asleep on the sofa when she got home from school. She flung her rucksack across the room at the sofa, where its flying plastic clips caught the back of my head. I flew into the air in panic, my hackles raised and my tail fluffed. She did not apologize for her clumsiness, nor did she even acknowledge my presence. As I tried to wash away my mortification afterwards, the thought crossed my mind that she had known I was there and had thrown her bag at me deliberately. I could not understand why Sophie would have a grudge against me, but her behaviour left me in no doubt that she disliked me.

Debbie had placed a cardboard shoebox in the café's bay window for me, which was where I often spent my mornings, observing the people who walked along the cobbled street in front of the café. The first to appear every day were grey-haired couples in waterproof coats and sensible shoes, on their way to the market square. Late morning was the time for young mums pushing buggies, with small children trailing behind them distractedly. Whenever the children noticed me in the window, they would drag their mothers over and point at me through the glass: 'Look, Mummy, cat!' and their mothers would smile wearily before pulling them away, with no time to dawdle.

There was one old woman who walked past the café on a daily basis, always wheeling a shopping trolley behind her. Something about her appearance perplexed me. Her posture and lined face reminded me of Margery, but rather than Margery's silvery-grey waves, the lady's hair was a strident reddish-brown, set fast around her head like a helmet. Her hair fascinated me as it never seemed to move, even when a strong wind was whipping up the canopies along the parade. Every time she saw me in the café window she scowled at me and, intrigued by her curious hair and angry expression, I would stare back.

Hardly any of the people who passed by on the street stepped foot inside the café, and it didn't escape my notice that the café attracted very few customers at all. A few workers from nearby shops and offices would pop in for a quick sandwich at lunchtime, but other than that it was not uncommon for the café to remain empty from dawn till dusk. I understood now why there had always been such generous quantities of leftovers in the dustbin in the alley. As an alley-cat, it had been a blessing, but now I realized that it had been a sign that the café was struggling.

Almost a week had passed before it even crossed my mind to go outside and return to the alley that had, until recently, been my home. There was no access to the alley from the flat, and Debbie did not like me using the kitchen door, so my only route in and out was through the café's front entrance. I waited till the café was about to close, reasoning that I would catch the tomcat as he came in search of the day's leftovers.

As soon as the church bells announced six o'clock, I slipped out of the café and around the corner to the alleyway. It was strange to see it again, through the eyes of a house-cat rather than a stray. I was struck by how exposed it was, and how draughty it felt, compared to the cosy flat up in the eaves. I sniffed the wall for the tom's scent marks, but there was no trace of him. I jumped onto the dustbin lid to look for the tell-tale rips in the rubbish bags that would indicate his presence, but the black polythene remained intact.

Puzzled, my tail twitched. Surely the tomcat would arrive soon, I figured, so I sat down on the dustbin to wait. I waited until my paws felt stiff with cold, but still he did not appear. It was only now that I understood how much I had been looking forward to seeing him again, and telling him everything that had happened since I had crossed the café's threshold. I was disappointed and hurt, feeling irrationally as if he had abandoned me. But my hurt quickly turned to guilt as I remembered the sudden nature of my departure, and that I had never told him of my plans. Had he wondered what had happened to me – maybe even worried for my safety? I felt a sharp pang of remorse for being so self-absorbed that I had not sought him out before now to explain what I had done.

I found my old sleeping place under the metal fire escape and settled down, determined to wait until he returned. But, apart from a squirrel dashing along the top of the dustbin, there was no sign of any other living thing in the alley apart from me. Eventually the café's back door opened and Debbie poked her head out. 'Molly, where are you? Here, puss.' I could hear alarm in her voice; this was the first time I had left the café since she had taken me in, and I had been out for hours.

For a moment I didn't know what to do: whether to stay out of sight under the fire escape and wait for the tomcat's return, or follow Debbie back into the warmth and security of the café. Debbie stepped out into the alley in her slippers, shivering with cold as she called my name again. I caught a glimpse of her face through the paint tins – a shadow of panic was plain to see in her eyes. My mind was made up. Regardless of what the tomcat might think of me, I couldn't bear to see Debbie so concerned for my well-being. I crawled out from the fire escape and trotted towards her, mewing in greeting. 'Oh, there you are, Molly!' she smiled. 'You naughty thing, I thought I'd lost you.'

She shepherded me quickly through the kitchen and I waited by the serving counter while she locked up. Sophie had gone out for the evening, so the flat was uncharacteristically quiet and peaceful. Debbie and I curled up side by side on the sofa, and she stroked me until we both began to nod off in front of the television, her bare feet cushioning my head. It felt just as I had imagined it would – an easy intimacy in which we were each soothed and reassured by the other's presence. And yet something niggled at the back of my mind, taking the edge off my happiness. It was the guilt I felt for the way I had treated the tomcat, for abandoning the alley with no thought for the impact it might have on him.

In Debbie, I had found everything I ever wanted, but my joy was tempered by the suspicion that, although I had undoubtedly gained much, I might have lost more than I realized.

17

It was Friday evening, one week exactly since I had moved into the café. Debbie was busy tidying the kitchen and I was in my box on the windowsill. I sat facing the street, but my eyes were closed as I reflected on the events of the past week, and how my life had been transformed by the simple act of crossing the café's threshold.

My meditations were interrupted by an insistent tapping above me. I jolted into alertness, quickly registering that a woman was standing in front of the window, rapping her knuckles on the glass. I looked up and immediately recognized the woman's unruly shoulder-length curls as belonging to Jo from the hardware shop. She was clutching a brown paper bag from the local takeaway in one hand, waving with the other to catch Debbie's attention. Debbie ran to the door and let her in.

'Evening, Debs. You took your time. I thought I was going to have to eat on the street!' She handed the bag to Debbie and unzipped her jacket.

I jumped down from the windowsill and trotted towards her. I had often seen Jo in the alley, but we had not yet been introduced. She lived in the flat upstairs from her shop with her ageing golden retriever, which spent its days dozing by her feet in the shop. In spite of the fact that she was a dog-owner, I liked Jo. She had a no-nonsense, practical air about her, and a humorous twinkle to her eye.

'So, this must be Molly from the alley,' Jo said, catching sight of me as I padded across the lino. She crouched down to greet me, giving me a cheerful rub on the back as I pressed against her leg. It was the kind of rub better suited to a dog than a cat, a little on the rough side, leaving my fur ruffled and messy, but I knew her intention was friendly, so I made no protest. I sniffed at her jeans, which smelt of dog, while she continued to scrutinize my appearance. Debbie had taken the bag of food into the kitchen and was retrieving plates and cutlery from the cupboards. 'You're right, Debs,' Jo called after her. 'She is a pretty little thing. Friendly, too.'

Debbie poked her head through the door, smiling at me indulgently, and I preened, basking in their attention.

'And you knew a big-hearted softy when you saw one, didn't you, Molly?' Jo whispered conspiratorially to me. 'A cute little face like yours – Debbie didn't stand a chance, did she?'

I purred, assuming the most innocent expression I could muster in defiance of Jo's knowing smile.

Jo stood up and walked over to the table where Debbie had begun to unpack their meal. Debbie placed the steaming foil trays side by side while Jo carefully removed their cardboard lids. The delicious smell of spicy meat began to fill the café, making my mouth water. Debbie returned to the kitchen to fetch a bottle of wine and two glasses, and at last they were ready to eat. As they sat down at the table, I returned to my position on the windowsill, tummy rumbling, to watch them.

'So how's Sophie?' Jo asked, while Debbie divided up the food onto their plates.

Debbie sighed. 'Not great. I know it's not easy for her, what with a new school, new people, a new home . . .' Her eyes started to well up.

Jo made a sympathetic noise and filled Debbie's wine glass. 'Has she heard from her dad?' Jo probed gently.

Debbie's face tightened. I had never heard her talk about Sophie's father. 'Not for a couple of weeks. He texted her to say he was going travelling with his girlfriend, and did she want anything from Duty Free?'

Jo winced, but Debbie's face remained a study of neutrality. She took a sip of wine, beginning to relax under Jo's supportive gaze.

'I know Sophie blames me for what happened,' Debbie said sadly. 'She thinks I decided to up sticks and move here just because I fancied it. But how can I explain it to her? He's her father – I've got to let her have the best relationship she can with him.'

'It's a tough one,' Jo agreed. 'It seems unfair, but . . . I guess you just have to let her work things out in her own time.' They ate in silence, Debbie's unhappiness almost tangible in the air. As she ate, Jo glanced at Debbie, registering her melancholy expression. 'So, do you want to hear about my latest romantic adventure?' she grinned, tilting her head coquettishly.

Debbie's face broke into a smile. 'Always!' she answered, leaning forward attentively in her chair.

'Well, I'm continuing to cut a swathe through Stourton's population of single men,' Jo began in mock-grandiosity, to Debbie's delighted giggling. She went on to describe a recent dinner date with a member of the Stourton Amateur Dramatic Society – 'SADS by name, sad by nature,' she said with a wink. The evening had started well; her date seemed rather pleased with himself, but other than that he was perfectly pleasant.

Jo paused for dramatic effect, taking a sip from her wine glass, as Debbie waited for the inevitable punchline. That was until pudding arrived, Jo went on, when her date had launched into an impromptu performance of a song from SADS' latest production. 'And let me tell you, Debbie,' she wagged a finger decisively, 'until you've been serenaded in a restaurant by a middle-aged man singing "A Modern Major General" – badly, I might add – you haven't lived!'

Debbie raised a hand to her mouth to stifle a laugh, while Jo helped herself to more wine. The alcohol in their drinks had begun to take effect; their facial expressions were becoming more exaggerated, their voices louder. 'There must be some eligible men in Stourton? Surely there's hope for us both?' Debbie asked, in half-sincere desperation.

'Oh, of course there are plenty,' Jo replied gravely. 'If it's a recently-retired member of the Lawn Bowls Society you're after, then you'll be spoilt for choice!'

Debbie snorted, then held up her glass in a toast. 'To the Lawn Bowls Society! I'll be signing up first thing tomorrow.'

Jo raised her glass and they both took a gulp of wine, their eyes glassy.

'In all seriousness, though, I doubt the Lawn Bowls Society would have me,' Debbie said morosely, slumping back in her chair. 'The good people of Stourton have made it very clear that I'm most definitely *not one of them.*'

Jo smiled sympathetically.

'We've been here six months, Jo, and apart from you I haven't made a single friend,' Debbie went on. 'It's like people don't trust us. There's one old crone who walks past here every day, and no matter how friendly I am, she doesn't say a word. Won't even smile.'

'I know,' Jo agreed, in a tone of resignation. 'The Stourton old guard will only grace your business with their custom if you've lived here for at least forty years. I've run the hardware shop since 1998 and some of them still won't step foot in it.' She was doing her best to reassure her friend but, judging from the doleful look on Debbie's face, it didn't seem to be working.

'But if I can't win round the locals, then I really am doomed,' Debbie despaired. 'I can't compete with all the foodie places round here, with their *artisan* this and *locally sourced* that. Don't Stourton people ever want a nice simple sandwich or baked potato for their lunch?'

By now she had consumed several glasses of wine and I could tell that her emotions were running high.

'I mean, is it really too much to ask of people – to give a local business a chance? Okay, it might not be a *sustainable, organic, locally sourced* sandwich, but that doesn't mean it's not a good sandwich.' Debbie looked flushed, and she paused to pour herself a glass of water.

'I know what you mean,' Jo replied. 'Personally, I wouldn't waste my money in any of those places. Give me a bacon roll any day.'

There was silence as Debbie gulped water from her glass. They had finished eating and Debbie placed the foil food trays on the floor, calling me over to devour the remnants of their creamy chicken curry and garlic prawns. Delighted, I jumped down and ran over to them. Debbie and Jo both laughed at my ravenousness as I greedily attacked the discarded prawn shells.

'Maybe the café just needs a unique selling point, Debs.' Jo's voice sounded forcibly upbeat. 'Something to make you stand out from the crowd.'

Debbie shrugged disconsolately. 'Maybe you're right,' she said flatly, looking unconvinced. 'How about *Debbie's Divorcee Diner? The only thing more bitter than our coffee is our clientele.*'

'Now there's an idea,' Jo laughed. 'I can see the full-page ad in the local paper already.'

Debbie smiled tipsily, topping up their glasses with the last of the wine.

'Chin up, Debs,' Jo said, taking a sip. 'Spring's just around the corner, the tourists will start to arrive soon and things'll pick up, I'm sure of it.'

'Thanks, Jo, perhaps you're right. That's if we haven't gone bankrupt by spring,' Debbie added ruefully.

It was almost midnight by the time Jo left. They

hugged and Debbie waved as Jo scuttled past the window back to her own flat. Debbie picked the foil food trays off the floor and cleared the table. Once she had finished in the kitchen, she made her way unsteadily round the café, flicking the lights off and struggling clumsily with the key as she locked the door. I followed a few paces behind as she climbed slowly up the stairs to the flat, swaying as she went. She leant her shoulder against the wall for a few seconds to regain her balance. 'Shhh, Molly, you'll wake Sophie!' she whispered loudly, and my tail twitched in indignation.

Debbie stumbled into the bathroom and I ran up the second flight of stairs to her bedroom to wait for her. I curled up on the end of her bed, mulling over the evening's conversation. Had Debbie been serious when she said the café might be bankrupt by spring? And if she was right, what would that mean for us? I pictured the café being closed down, and Debbie tearfully telling me that she couldn't look after me any more. I began to wash, trying to push thoughts of such an unhappy scenario from my mind.

I was acutely aware that my ability to be of any practical help to Debbie was minimal. Just as I had been unable to prevent Margery's illness from enveloping her mind, so I was equally powerless to turn around the fortunes of the café. All I could do for Debbie was what I had done for Margery: hope that my presence brought her some comfort, and pray that things were going to be okay.

Debbie emerged from the bathroom smelling of toothpaste and soap. She wearily changed into her pyjamas, throwing her clothes across the bed onto a chair by the window. They missed, sliding to the floor in a heap. Debbie groaned and looked at the clothes guiltily for a moment. 'Never mind, sort it out tomorrow,' she slurred under her breath, before climbing into bed and switching off the bedside light. The room took on an ethereal quality as a shaft of moonlight illuminated the silvery tones of the quilt. I padded up the bed and nudged Debbie's side with my nose. One arm was draped across her forehead, but she began to stroke me sleepily with her other hand.

'Oh, Molly,' she sighed. 'So much for a fresh start. The café's losing money hand over fist, and my daughter hates me.'

Her hand dropped limply onto the cover in front of me, and I began to lick it gently. Her eyes were closed, but Debbie smiled weakly and moved her fingers to tickle me under the chin. 'Still, I suppose it's not all bad,' she mumbled drowsily. 'At least I found you, Molly.' Debbie's hand fell still, but I continued to lick her fingers, listening as her breathing became slower and deeper and she sank into sleep. Once I was certain she was asleep, I continued with my own wash, tasting the lingering scent of Debbie's skin on my fur.

As I washed, it occurred to me for the first time how much Debbie and I had in common. Not that she knew it, of course, but I was also an outsider in Stourton. I had come to the town in the hope of a fresh start too and, like Debbie, I knew what it was like to feel unwelcome here.

Memories of my first night in Stourton came unbidden to mind. I vividly recalled the desperate loneliness I had felt as people rushed past me on the market square, preoccupied with their last-minute Christmas shopping. Being surrounded by people, yet feeling unnoticed and unloved, had been far harder than fending for myself in the countryside. In town, there was no escaping the fact that it was an owner that I longed for – someone to care for me and take me home. The trauma of being attacked by the alley-cat had compounded my feeling of desolation. I had felt completely alone: invisible to the humans of Stourton, and viewed as a rival by its felines.

Watching Debbie as she slept, I wondered if she felt the same way about Stourton as I had: that at best it was indifferent to her, and at worst it resented her presence. I dearly wished I could tell Debbie that I knew how she felt, or reassure her that she would find a way through it, just as I had. I had survived in the alley after all, living on my wits until Debbie had taken me in. But, as I thought about my life in the alley, I felt a familiar stirring of guilt. It was true that I had been ownerless, but I had not been alone out there. The tomcat had made sure, in his unassuming way, that I knew there was somewhere I could find food and shelter, somewhere that was safe from the vicious alley-cats. I felt a swell of gratitude to him, followed by a pang of remorse that I had repaid his kindness by moving inside as soon as I had the chance.

I had been back out to the alley to look for him again on several occasions since my first attempt. Each time I was optimistic, convinced I would catch sight of his tail disappearing through the conifers or his green eyes lurking in the shadows, but each time I was disappointed. The alley was silent and uninhabited. He had vanished without a trace.

Debbie was deep in sleep now and her face was relaxed in a way I rarely saw when she was awake. I finished my wash and lowered my chin onto my paws, reflecting on everything she had done for me. She had given me a home, but she had also given me a purpose; she was struggling too, and I knew she needed me. I would always regret the way I had treated the tomcat, but from now on Debbie had to be my priority.

18

In addition to feeling like outsiders in Stourton, Debbie and I had something else in common: Sophie appeared to hate us both. Debbie always started the day with the best intentions, waking Sophie for school by singing 'Oh, What a Beautiful Morning' as she pulled open the bedroom curtains. 'Leave me alone,' Sophie would shout from under the covers, establishing a mood of determined sulkiness, which she would maintain for the rest of the day.

Sophie was never far from her mobile phone; she even slept with it under her pillow. With headphones permanently in her ears, she was oblivious to everything around her, and Debbie seemed resigned to the fact that she had to repeat herself at least three times before her daughter heard anything she said. Other than her phone, however, Sophie showed a total disregard for her belongings. She left her clothes in piles on the bedroom floor and allowed her school books to get trodden underfoot, in spite of Debbie's repeated pleas for her to take more care.

Sophie's rage seemed to be triggered by the slightest thing I did. She was revolted by the smell of my food, horrified by my moulting fur and mortally offended if she even caught me looking at her. 'Why does that cat always stare at me?' she complained at the table one evening, carrying her food upstairs to her bedroom and leaving Debbie, in stunned silence, to finish dinner alone.

One of my early attempts to win Sophie round backfired miserably. Early one morning I found a mouse scurrying inside the fireplace in the living room. I dispatched it swiftly, before picking it up carefully between my jaws and carrying it upstairs to the attic. Sophie was still asleep in bed, so I crept silently into her room and placed the still-warm mouse on a dirty plate she had left on the floor. As I tiptoed out onto the landing I felt a glow of satisfaction. Surely, if Sophie wanted a sign that somebody cared for her, this ought to do the job?

I joined Debbie in the little kitchen, where she was making herself a cup of tea. She had just poured the milk when we heard a blood-curdling shriek from above.

'Sophie? What on earth's the matter?' Debbie called.

Sophie appeared at the end of the hallway, pulling on her school uniform. 'That. Cat. Is. Gross,' she hissed as she pushed past us. 'And I am *not* cleaning it up!' she added, plugging in her headphones and running downstairs.

We heard the café door slam and Debbie looked at me questioningly. Ashamed of what I had done, I could hardly bear to meet her gaze and slunk into the living room. I heard Debbie move around in Sophie's room upstairs, trying to make some order in the mess. A short while later she reappeared in the living room, clutching a plastic bag with the remains of the dead mouse inside. I looked at the bag sheepishly, waiting for a telling-off. 'Don't worry, Molly, it was a lovely thought,' Debbie said supportively. 'But no more gifts for Sophie, please.'

As I tried to find a space on the sofa amidst the dirty contents of her PE kit, I wondered whether Sophie's problem was, in feline terms, a territory issue. Perhaps, like an alley-cat, she needed to feel in control of her surroundings, and saw me as a territorial rival. Certainly, much of her frustration was directed at the flat itself. She took issue with everything, from the size of her bedroom to the poor Wi-Fi signal. The balled-up dirty socks that she had left on the cushion seemed to me to serve the same purpose as a cat's scent-marker: they let everyone know that she had been there, reminding us of her presence even when she wasn't around.

One weeknight, over dinner, Debbie politely enquired how Sophie's day had been.

'Crap, as usual,' Sophie answered bluntly. I had heard her tell Debbie on many occasions that she missed her friends from her old school and wished they had never left Oxford.

Debbie sighed wearily, and I braced myself for the row that would inevitably follow.

'Look, Sophie, I know it's hard for you, but give it time. We've both got to find our feet here.' She looked at Sophie pleadingly. 'It's not easy for me, either.' The reference to her own difficulties ignited Sophie's fury.

'Not easy for you?' she repeated sarcastically, her face starting to redden. 'At least you've got Jo and that . . . mangy fleabag' – she pointed at me – 'I haven't got *one single friend* in this town. And it's all thanks to you and your *fresh start.*'

'Her name is Molly, Sophie, and she doesn't have fleas,' Debbie replied, trying to keep her voice steady.

I had heard Debbie and Sophie row on many occasions, but this was the first time I had become the subject of one of their arguments, and I felt excruciatingly uncomfortable. I didn't want to hear a detailed account of Sophie's many grievances against me, so I jumped off the sofa and crept out of the room, not wanting to inflame the situation any further by my presence. I walked across the hallway to the kitchen, where I ate a few dry cat biscuits disconsolately.

In the living room Debbie was making every effort not to get drawn into a shouting match, knowing that, if she did, it would end in the same way as all their previous rows: with Sophie storming out of the flat. When she finally spoke, Debbie's voice was low and calm.

'Look, Soph, you're angry, I get that. You didn't want to leave Oxford, and I get that, too. But we're here now, and I'm asking – begging – you to accept that I made what I thought was the right choice for us. Not because I wanted a fresh start, but because there was no alternative.'

I crossed the hallway and peered around the living-room door. Sophie was sitting on a dining chair with her shoulders slumped, staring at the carpet. Debbie stood in front of her, her hands on her hips. 'But you're right,' Debbie went on. 'I have got Jo, and I've got Molly, but maybe that's because I was open to the idea of making friends. You never know, Sophie, it might work for you too, if you try it.'

Sophie was staring at the carpet defiantly, refusing to look at her mother's face as she talked.

Debbie's cheeks were flushed, and I could see how

much she wanted Sophie to say something – anything – to acknowledge that she had heard her. I pondered the workings of the human mind. I couldn't fathom why, if Sophie was jealous of Debbie's affection for me, she made it so difficult for her mother to love her. Her anger was pushing Debbie away, creating a breach between them that was in danger of becoming irreparable.

'Let's not make life any harder for ourselves by fighting all the time. Please?' Debbie's voice was desperate, but Sophie remained stubbornly silent. Debbie stepped forward to tuck a messy strand of hair out of Sophie's face, but Sophie batted her hand away. She turned towards the door to avoid Debbie's gaze and I caught sight of her eyes, which were red and watery. Within seconds she had grabbed her phone from the table and walked past me, out into the hall. Debbie remained in the living room, waiting for the sound of Sophie's footsteps running downstairs. But instead Sophie walked to the other end of the hall and climbed the stairs to the attic, slamming her bedroom door behind her.

Debbie puffed out her cheeks and looked up at the ceiling. I walked over to her and leant against her leg in a show of moral support that I knew would be of little help. Debbie slowly cleared the table, emptying Sophie's half-eaten meal into the bin and washing up the dirty plates. Then, although it was still early, she turned off the lights in the flat and, without saying goodnight to me, went upstairs to her own bedroom.

I sat in the hallway feeling helpless and confused. I had been relieved that the row had not ended with Sophie storming out, but the pain that seemed to emanate from both of them almost felt worse. It was as if they'd reached a stalemate, and neither of them could see a way out. Based on the way she had treated me, I had no reason to like Sophie, but I knew that Debbie could never be happy unless her daughter was happy too. But while Sophie remained convinced I was part of the problem, it seemed beyond my feline powers to help her.

19

'Mum, why is there no hot water?'

It was the morning after the argument. Sophie was running the shower in the bathroom as she got ready for school. I stepped out of the living room to find Debbie standing in the hall touching a radiator, an anxious look on her face. 'Mum!' Sophie shouted impatiently.

'I don't know, Sophie. It must be the boiler. The radiators aren't working, either.' Debbie sounded worried, and I could feel the chill in the flat as the residual warmth in the radiators drained away.

Sophie was even more bad-tempered than usual that morning. Having been unable to shower, she acted as though Debbie was responsible for her unwashed hair and freezing bedroom. When Debbie ran downstairs to look at the boiler in the café kitchen I followed her, keen not to become the next object of Sophie's annoyance.

Debbie was standing in the kitchen talking on the phone. 'I haven't got a clue, Jo. The pilot light's gone out and there's a fault code on the display, but I can't find the manual.' She was rifling through drawers, desperately pulling out yellowing instruction booklets and old takeaway menus. While Jo talked at the other end of the line, Debbie grabbed a pen and scribbled something on the back of a pizza menu. 'That's great, thanks, Jo. I'll give him a call.'

Sophie thundered down the stairs and through the kitchen, running late for her bus.

'Bye, love, have a good—' Debbie called after her, but Sophie had slammed the door shut before she could finish. 'Calm – stay calm,' Debbie muttered to herself, picking up the phone to dial the number Jo had given her.

About half an hour later I watched from the windowsill as a van pulled up on the cobbles outside the café. A tall, sandy-haired man got out and pulled a bag onto his shoulder before knocking on the door.

'Thank God you're here!' Debbie exclaimed as she unlocked the café and ushered him in.

'I wish all my clients greeted me like that,' he said, smiling. 'I'm John. So your boiler's playing up?'

'That's right: the light's gone out – there's no

water . . .' Debbie stammered as she led him into the kitchen.

Through the doorway I could see her perched on a stool, drumming her fingers nervously on the worktop while John began to take the boiler apart. His manner remained calm, in spite of Debbie's evident alarm.

'Boilers always pick the worst time to pack up, don't they?' John said, sensing her anxiety. Debbie smiled tensely. 'It's a bit of an antique, this model – must be at least thirty years old,' he added.

Debbie was unable to contain her impatience any longer. 'Well, what do you think?' she asked.

'It's not great news, I'm afraid,' John replied, looking genuinely sorry. 'You've had a leak inside. Water's been dripping onto the casing. It's completely corroded in here.'

Debbie stood next to him and peered into the boiler to see the damage for herself.

'I can patch it up for now, but it's only a short-term solution. You're going to need a new boiler, I'm afraid.'

Debbie groaned and sat back down on her stool, her head sinking. I couldn't see her face clearly from the window, but I could picture her look of reluctant acceptance. She took a deep breath and closed her eyes. 'Right. Okay. If you could do what you can for now, that would be great. I'm going to have to speak to the bank.'

John nodded respectfully and went to fetch his tools from the van. As he walked back into the café he noticed me for the first time. 'Hello, puss,' he smiled, making a detour across the café to give me a stroke.

My interest was piqued and I stood up to greet him. As he approached me I noticed that his sandy hair bore a few streaks of grey and the bridge of his nose was dusted with freckles. As he held out a hand to stroke me, the corners of his eyes crinkled into a smile. I leant forwards to sniff his fingers, and he tousled my ears teasingly. I responded to his playfulness by wrapping my front paws around his wrist, gripping his skin with my claws and biting the side of his thumb.

'You don't want to let me go, do you?' he laughed, wincing in pain as he tried to twist his arm free. 'And it's not often I get to say that!'

I noticed Debbie watching us from the kitchen doorway and, expecting to be told off, I loosened my grip. As she walked towards us, however, I was surprised to see that her look of concern had been replaced by an indulgent smile. 'That's Molly,' she said, and she explained how she had found me in the alley and taken me in.

'And now she thinks she owns the place, by the look of it,' John joked, and Debbie tilted her head in agreement.

John gave me a final rub behind the ears before

setting to work on the boiler. I lay down in my shoebox, listening as he and Debbie chatted. He had grown up in Stourton, he told her. It had changed a lot since his childhood, what with all the second-home owners and the rise in property prices. A lot of the shops in Stourton were still family businesses, though, and had stayed in the same family for generations.

'This place was empty for a while, if I remember rightly,' he said. 'How long have you been here?'

'Coming up to six months,' Debbie replied. 'We were in Oxford before. I've never run a café before and it's been a . . . learning curve.'

John smiled. 'I remember coming here when I was a kid. It was a greasy spoon back then. Although' – he peered through the kitchen doorway to the café – 'it hasn't changed all that much since then. I'm sure that's been here for at least thirty years!' He was looking at the ugly serving counter.

'Oh, has it really?' Debbie replied, looking aghast at the metal-and-plastic construction. She scanned the café's interior unhappily. 'I suppose the whole place could do with a bit of an update, now that you mention it.'

I had been absorbed in observing the two of them, but a movement on the street caught my eye. Sophie was striding along the cobbles, heading home for lunch. As she crossed the street in front of the café she stopped, distracted by something. The old lady with the shopping trolley and curiously coloured hair was on the other side of the street and had said something to her. Sophie pulled a headphone out of one ear, a frown forming as she listened. It was all over in a matter of seconds and then the old lady was on her way again, the wheels of her shopping trolley rattling over the cobbles.

When she pushed open the café door, Sophie's face was furious.

'Oh, hi, Soph. We've got hot water again if you want a . . . shower . . .' Debbie had stepped out of the kitchen to greet her, but Sophie barged past, heading straight for the stairs. 'What's wrong, love?' Debbie called, but the only answer was the sound of a door slamming upstairs. Debbie looked at the floor, embarrassed.

'Teenagers, eh?' John said sympathetically when she returned to the kitchen, and Debbie managed a weak smile.

He had done what he could and began to pack his tools away. I wandered across the café to sniff at his bag, while Debbie made out a cheque for the work. She was full of gratitude and promised to be in touch soon about replacing the boiler.

John opened his mouth as if to say something, but then paused, leaving an awkward silence hanging in the air. He caught sight of me on the floor next to his bag. 'Bye, Molly, look after the place, won't you?' he said, giving me a quick stroke as he lifted the bag to his shoulder.

As he was leaving he popped his head back through the door.

'You know, I'm sure I could get that stove working for you, if you ever decide to do the place up.'

'Thanks,' Debbie replied thoughtfully. 'I might take you up on that.'

John left, and for a moment Debbie's eyes lingered on the door after it had closed behind him.

'You know what, Molly, I think he's right. This place needs a facelift. And that monstrosity has *got* to go,' she said, eyeing the serving counter with disgust.

Part of me wanted to say that I could have told her that weeks ago, but I thought it was enough to purr encouragingly. After her stressful morning it was good to see a sparkle back in Debbie's eyes, although whether that was down to the thought of doing up the café or something else entirely, I wasn't sure.

20

Debbie arranged for someone to mind the café so that she could spend the following day looking into the business finances. She carried several heavy folders into the living room and spread them across the table, then sat down with a heavy sigh. She had tied her hair back in a ponytail, and reading glasses were perched on her nose as she worked her way through the piles of paper in front of her. During the course of the morning she made numerous lengthy phone calls enquiring about business-development loans and interest rates, and sat listlessly as recorded music was played down the telephone line. Making a show of supportiveness, I sat on the dining table to keep her company, but before long I had dozed off in an empty foolscap box-file.

Debbie was still engrossed in her work when Sophie got home from school. 'Hello, love. Gosh, is that the time already?' she said, looking up, startled.

She stretched back in her chair, rolling her head from side to side to relieve the tension in her neck. 'Tell you what, Soph, why don't I make us both a cup of tea? I could do with a break from all these numbers.'

Sophie was hovering indecisively in the doorway. Her rucksack was still slung over her shoulder, and I eyed it nervously lest her mood turned and she decided to fling it at me. 'Yeah, okay,' she replied, placing her bag and jacket on one of the dining chairs.

Debbie disappeared into the kitchen, emerging a few minutes later with two mugs of tea and a packet of chocolate biscuits, which she waved in front of Sophie's nose. 'I think we've earned these, don't you?' she said, opening the packet and offering it to her daughter. Sophie smiled and took a biscuit.

'So, how was school?' Debbie asked, a flicker of concern in her eyes as she broached what she knew to be a delicate subject.

Sophie shrugged, taking a bite out of a chocolate chip cookie. 'Dunno,' she answered vaguely. Debbie smiled, patiently waiting while Sophie finished her mouthful. 'My form tutor's still a moron,' Sophie volunteered, taking a second bite. Debbie smiled sympathetically. 'But I sat next to Jade on the bus home, and she said the whole school knows he's an utter—' Debbie's eyebrows had shot up and Sophie stopped herself, pausing to choose her words. 'He's an *unpopular* teacher,' she said carefully, smirking across the rim of her mug.

This was the most information Sophie had disclosed about her school life in all the time I had known her, and I sensed that Debbie wanted to capitalize on her openness. 'Does Jade live in Stourton too?' she probed, casually sipping her tea.

Sophie nodded. 'Yeah. I might meet her in town this weekend actually.' She had picked up her phone and started to scroll through a backlog of text messages on her screen.

Sensing that her daughter's interest had wandered elsewhere, Debbie patted her on the arm as she stood up to clear the empty biscuit packet. 'Sounds like a good idea – the two of you could get a milkshake together.'

Sophie shot Debbie a withering look. 'Yeah, all right, Mum. We're not five years old, you know.'

Debbie lifted her hands in a gesture of submission. 'Of course not, love. I didn't mean to suggest—' She stopped, relieved to see that Sophie was smiling at her.

There were further phone calls during the week as Debbie got the finances in place to pay for the planned refurbishment of the café. On Friday evening Sophie reluctantly agreed to help her move the furniture, stacking the chairs and tables inside the kitchen and clearing the serving counter. The sight of the empty café made me melancholy. It reminded me of Margery's house when it was being packed up, and the sadness I had felt at seeing empty floor where once there had been furniture, and marks on the walls where pictures had hung. I did not want to linger downstairs any longer than necessary, and happily ran up to bed with Debbie as soon as she had locked up.

First thing on Saturday morning I heard the bell above the café door tinkle. It was Jo. 'Right, boss. What's first?' she asked cheerily.

Debbie had got up early and was already kneeling on the floor next to the stove. 'Hi, Jo. Help me get this lino up, would you?' she answered. 'John's coming later to have a look at the stove, so I want to get the fireplace area cleared.'

Jo took off her coat and hung it up, while Debbie started to score at the floor with a Stanley knife.

'So John's coming to help? Well, isn't that kind of him? And on a weekend, too.'

Something about Jo's tone made Debbie look up. 'And what's that face for?' Debbie said drily, running the blade sharply along the floor.

'What face? I'm not making a face,' Jo replied innocently. 'I'm merely thinking how kind it is of John to give up his weekend to fix your stove.' A mischievous smile played around her lips.

'Well, you're not here to think – you're here to work,' Debbie replied curtly. 'But for your information, he's not doing it out of kindness. I will be recompensing him for his time.'

'I'm sure you will,' Jo muttered under her breath, which Debbie pretended not to hear.

Although Debbie had removed all the furniture from the café, she had left my box on the windowsill. I climbed into it and watched as they moved slowly across the café floor, scoring the lino before ripping it up in jagged sections. After a couple of hours they both looked hot and flustered. Debbie crawled on her hands and knees to the stairs.

'Soph! Please, love, take pity on two old women and put the kettle on!' Sophie grunted in response, and a few minutes later she appeared at the bottom of the stairs carrying two mugs of tea. Jo and Debbie gratefully took a mug each, then collapsed side by side on the bare floor, their backs against the wall.

'I'm meeting Jade, Mum. See you later,' Sophie said, picking her way between their outstretched legs on her way to the door.

'See you later, love,' Debbie called, blowing her a kiss.

Debbie and Jo were sipping tea in silence when John pushed the café door open. 'Morning, ladies. Hard at it, I see.'

They shot him withering looks, and soon John was set to work fixing the stove, while Debbie and Jo discussed how best to dismantle the serving counter. I suspected it was going to be a noisy and dusty afternoon, so I decided to leave them to it and head upstairs to sleep off my low mood in the flat.

The smell of takeaway food drifting up the stairs woke me. Night had fallen and I could hear Debbie and Jo chatting as they dragged a table and chairs across the café. Sophie must have returned home during the afternoon, as I found her half-heartedly rooting around inside the fridge. When Debbie called up to ask her if she fancied joining them for a curry, Sophie shouted back, 'Yeah, okay,' without hesitation.

Not wanting to be left out, I followed Sophie downstairs. The café looked completely different from when I had last seen it. The grey lino had gone, revealing handsome flagstones underneath, and the serving counter had also been removed, exposing a wide section of floor that had not seen the light of day for decades. John had gone, but the stove in the fireplace was working, a healthy yellow flame flickering inside the blackened glass door. In spite of its emptiness, the café felt imbued by the warm firelight with a cosy intimacy. Even Sophie seemed momentarily taken aback, pausing on the bottom step to take in the transformation.

'Well, Soph? Looking better already, don't you think?' Debbie asked. Her overalls were covered in dust and thick strands of hair had slipped out of her pony-tail.

Sophie had headphones in her ears, but nodded in agreement. Debbie pulled a chair up to the table for Sophie, and Jo handed her a plate. 'Thanks,' she mumbled under her breath, spooning out some rice and a little curry.

'What do you think of the tiles, Sophie?' Jo asked her, gesturing proudly to the flagstones.

'Dunno, could do with a clean, I suppose,' Sophie answered noncommittally.

Jo pretended to take offence. 'She's a chip off the old block, isn't she?' she said to Debbie. 'You work your fingers to the bone, and all she does is complain about the dirt! You're as bad as your mother, Sophie!'

Sophie looked chastened and regretful. 'Sorry, I didn't mean it like that.'

'Don't worry, Sophie,' Debbie cut in. 'She's just pulling your leg, aren't you, Jo?'

Jo grinned, and Sophie surreptitiously slipped her headphones out of her ears, placing her phone on the table. 'Fire's nice,' she said, chewing a mouthful of curry.

The three of them looked towards the stove, where I had wasted no time in stretching out to bask in its warm glow. 'It certainly looks like Molly approves,' Debbie chuckled.

Debbie and Jo ate ravenously after the day's exertions and, with Sophie picking at the food as well, I began to despair of there being any leftovers for me. Although I had spent a quiet day indoors, I was unusually hungry. I waited patiently for them all to finish, and eventually Debbie put the foil trays on the floor for me to lick. She cleared away the plates, and when she returned from the kitchen she was clutching a paint chart.

'Right, ladies, your assistance is required. I need to choose a colour for the walls, and can't decide between *Mouse's Breath*, *Smoked Mackerel* and *Drizzle*. What do you think?'

Debbie held up the chart in front of them. Jo wrinkled her nose uncertainly and Sophie looked nonplussed.

'Mum, they're all horrible,' she said. 'Mousy-grey, fishy-grey or rainy-grey. Urgh!'

Debbie looked downcast, and turned to Jo for backup. 'I thought they were muted and tasteful. Very Stourton. Don't you agree, Jo?'

Jo avoided her gaze. 'Pass it here,' she said, sidestepping the question. She put her hand out to take the chart from Debbie. 'They may be very Stourton, but

I think Sophie's right. There must be something here with a bit more colour.'

Jo unfolded the chart, holding it up to the light every now and then. 'Aha!' she exclaimed. 'Surely this has to be the one!' She turned the chart towards the others and pointed at a square of pale pink.

'I suppose it's nice,' Debbie said half-heartedly, still smarting from the unanimous dismissal of her favoured shades.

'You don't sound too sure, Debs, but you know what's going to clinch the deal for you? It's called *Molly's Blushes*.'

At the sound of my name I looked up from the empty foil tray, which I had been licking across the floor.

Debbie took the paint chart for a closer look. 'I suppose pink might make the place look friendly,' she said uncertainly. 'What do you think, Soph?'

Sophie shrugged. 'Yeah, it's all right, I s'pose. Better than grey, at least.'

Debbie frowned at the chart thoughtfully. 'Yes, okay, why not? Everyone likes pink, right?' she said decisively, her frown giving way to a smile.

'That settles it!' Jo announced, pouring out two glasses of wine. 'To *Molly's Blushes*! Here's to a fun-packed day of painting tomorrow.'

'*Molly's Blushes*!' Debbie repeated, clinking her glass

against Jo's. 'Come on, Soph, join in – it's a toast,' she chided.

Sophie rolled her eyes and reluctantly lifted her glass of water. '*Molly's Blushes,*' she mumbled self-consciously.

They all looked at me as they sipped their drinks, and I was relieved that none of them could see my actual blushes through my fur.

21

Debbie was standing in the kitchen, waiting for the kettle to boil. She and Jo had shared a bottle of wine with their takeaway meal and judging by Debbie's puffy eyes and pallid skin this morning, they had opened a second bottle. I was hungry but, seeing her fragile state, decided to wait until Debbie had a cup of tea in her hand before mewing for my breakfast. She pulled the fridge door open and peered inside, letting out a loud groan.

'Soph! Did you finish the milk last night?' she called huskily.

'Might've,' Sophie replied vaguely from inside the bathroom. 'I had a bowl of cereal at bedtime.'

Debbie closed the fridge and pressed her forehead against the door with a pained expression. 'There's no milk left and I have a half-made cup of tea in front of me. Could you please pop out and get a pint?'

'What?' Sophie yelled over the sound of running water.

'I said' – Debbie was shouting now – 'since you finished the milk, could you please go and buy some more?' She winced in pain at the sound of her own voice.

The water pipes fell silent as Sophie turned off the taps. Debbie emptied her mug of half-made tea into the sink and rubbed her face, catching sight of me at last as I sat patiently in the doorway. 'All right, Molly, I know. You want feeding, don't you?'

I stood next to my dish while she squeezed out a cat-food pouch, starting to gag when some of the meaty liquid dribbled over her fingers. 'Urgh, I feel sick,' she moaned, rinsing her hand under the kitchen tap, as I tucked happily into my breakfast.

While I was eating, Sophie appeared in the doorway. She had pulled jeans and a hoodie over her pyjamas and was clumsily stuffing bare feet into a pair of trainers.

'Thanks, love,' Debbie said, handing her some money.

Sophie grunted and ran downstairs. I followed her out, slipping through the café door behind her.

I rarely ventured further than the alleyway and churchyard on my excursions out of the café, but early on a Sunday morning was a good time to roam further afield. The air smelt sweet and clean, untainted by the fumes of passing traffic, and the narrow streets were peaceful, devoid of shoppers and tourists. Sophie turned left, heading for the market square, but I set off in the other direction. I meandered along the quiet cobbled streets, pausing to watch as a group of Lycra-clad cyclists sped past. In the brilliant sunshine of early spring it was difficult to imagine that vicious alley-cats lurked in hidden passageways, and yet I made sure to give a wide berth to every alley I passed.

As I made my way back along the cobbles towards the cafe I saw a figure standing in front of the bay window. She had one hand pressed against the glass, shading her eyes from the bright reflection as she peered inside. Dropping to my haunches, I crept closer, my hackles rising as soon as I noticed the familiar shopping trolley by her side. When I was a couple of feet away, the old woman noticed my movement at the edge of her vision and spun round to face me. Sensing hostility and alert to possible danger, I stopped mid-step, one paw hovering off the ground, tail twitching as she glared at me across the cobbles.

Without saying a word, the old woman grabbed her shopping trolley and thrust it forward with both hands. Its wheels scraped on the ground as it lunged towards me. I darted effortlessly out of its path and watched the trolley wobble, before falling sideways, landing on the street with a thud.

'Hey, what do you think you're doing?'

The woman and I both turned in the direction of the voice. Sophie was walking up the street, a pint of milk in one hand. Her hood was pulled up, but I could make out her angry expression underneath. In my confusion I assumed that her words were addressed to me, but to my surprise the old lady answered. 'I'm . . . I'm not doing anything – it . . . it slipped,' she stuttered defensively.

Sophie strode towards her with a look of incipient fury and the old woman began to shuffle backwards. The alarming thought crossed my mind that I was about to witness a physical assault. When Sophie reached the upturned shopping trolley, however, she stopped. I instinctively stepped behind her ankles for protection. 'Haven't you got anything better to do with your time than try to hurt people's pets?' Sophie demanded.

'It just fell over. I didn't mean to . . . ' the woman muttered, unconvincingly.

Sophie lifted up the shopping trolley by its handle, standing it upright in front of its owner. 'Well, it's not fallen over any more, is it? So you can go now.'

The woman mumbled something indistinct that might have been an apology. Without looking at Sophie, she grabbed her trolley by the handle and turned to leave.

'Nosy old witch,' Sophie muttered as we watched her scurry away down the street. To my surprise, she then bent down and stroked me. 'Don't worry about her, Molly. She can't hurt you.'

The whole incident left me baffled and unsettled. I had become accustomed to the way the old woman scowled at me through the window, but it had never crossed my mind that she might want to hurt me. Bad-tempered but harmless was what I had considered her, but Sophie's reaction made me wonder if I had under-estimated her. My disquiet about the old woman was offset, however, by the turnaround in Sophie's attitude towards me. After so many weeks of antagonism, to feel protected by Sophie was a joyous relief. I purred as she stroked me, arching my back and rising onto my tiptoes at the touch of her hand.

I stayed close to Sophie's ankles as she pushed the café door open.

'Got the milk, Mum,' she shouted, and Debbie came downstairs, dressed in her decorating overalls with her hair tied back. Full of gratitude, she took the milk and disappeared into the café kitchen, while Sophie loped upstairs to the flat.

I jumped up onto the café windowsill to wash and think. Why had Sophie not mentioned the incident outside to Debbie? And why had the old lady tried to mow me down with her trolley in the first place? I recalled the time I had seen her accost Sophie outside the shop, and the look of angry indignation on Sophie's face afterwards. She hadn't told Debbie about that, either. I began to wonder if there was more going on with the old woman than I had realized and if, unwittingly, it involved me.

My thoughts were interrupted by the sound of the café door opening. It was Jo, carrying two large paint tins. 'Four litres of *Molly's Blushes!*' she announced. 'Just the thing for a hangover, eh, Debs?'

Clutching her mug of tea at last, Debbie turned on the radio and soon she and Jo were happily rolling paint onto the walls, transforming them from dirty white to warm pink. I prowled around the café while they worked, playing with some crinkly cellophane wrapping that I found in the fireplace.

After a while I began to feel light-headed. I had been fighting a nagging queasiness all morning, which I attributed to the paint fumes. I sat down at the bottom of the stairs, trying to master my discomfort, when two things happened at once: Sophie ran down the stairs behind me, and Jo dropped the lid from a tin of paint, sending it clattering to the floor. Panicked, my fight-or-flight instinct kicked in. I bolted towards the café door but, in my nauseous state, it was not until I reached the doorstep that I noticed that it was shut. I turned on my heels and made for the windowsill. It was as I leapt up onto it that I heard Debbie shout, 'No, Molly – stop!'

Only then did I become aware of the sensation of wetness underneath my paws. I sat down on the windowsill and lifted up my front pad. I could smell a strong chemical odour, and saw that my paw was dripping with pink paint. A quick check confirmed that my other paws were similarly affected. I looked across the café, noticing for the first time the plastic paint-tray that Debbie had placed on the floor near the stairs. In my panic I had run straight through it, leaving a trail of pink paw prints behind me on the flagstones.

'Oh, Molly!' Debbie sighed, her voice a mixture of irritation and concern.

I looked at her sheepishly.

Jo started laughing, a nasal snigger that she tried to stifle, but which soon turned into a throaty cackle. 'So much for *Molly's Blushes.*' She said. '*Molly's Footprints* would be more accurate.' Sophie, who had watched the scene unfold from the bottom of the stairs, started to giggle too.

Seeing the reaction of the other two, Debbie couldn't help but smile. I lifted one my paws to start licking off the paint. 'Oh, don't let her lick them!' Debbie cried.

Sophie sprang across the café and sat down next to me in the window, trying to distract me from the urge to clean my dirty paws. Meanwhile Debbie ran into the kitchen, emerging with a damp cloth.

'Hold her still, will you, Soph?'

Sophie gripped me gently by the shoulders, while Debbie lifted each paw in turn to wipe the paint from them.

'You know what, Deb – I reckon you should keep them,' said Jo, looking at the trail of pink paw prints. 'They actually look pretty cool. They can be a *design feature.*'

'Yeah, right,' Debbie laughed.

'She's right, Mum,' Sophie agreed. 'Keep them. They're funny.'

Debbie had finished wiping my feet and looked at the pink trail that criss-crossed the floor. 'Seriously?' she repeated, as if she suspected they were both in on the same joke.

'Why not?' Jo replied. 'You wanted to stand out from the crowd, didn't you? I bet there aren't any other cafés in Stourton with their very own paw-print trail.'

Debbie looked unconvinced, and stood up to take the cloth back to the kitchen.

The smell of paint on my paws had intensified my queasiness. I jumped down from the window and picked a careful route across the café, avoiding the trail of damp prints. Desperate for some fresh air, I stood at the door hoping to catch somebody's attention. 'Would you like to go out, Molly?' Sophie asked, her voice sounding uncannily like her mother's. I chirruped gratefully as she pulled the café door open for me.

I stepped out onto the doorstep and took a few deep breaths of spring air, allowing the sun's rays to warm my face. I sat for a while on the pavement outside the café, waiting for the queasiness to pass, before heading to the alley behind the café. It was silent but for the cooing of pigeons in the eaves and the chattering crows building their nests in the churchyard treetops. Although it still held painful memories for me, I felt a feeling of peace and well-being as I contemplated the empty alley. It was impossible not to think about the tomcat as I stood in the place that had been our shared home; but, rather than the usual sadness and guilt, I felt the glimmering of something positive inside. Maybe it was an acceptance that he had gone, or perhaps it was just an acknowledgement that, finally, life seemed to be settling down, after months of upheaval.

I crept over to my old hiding place under the fire escape, curious to see if it had changed since I had last used it, in the depths of winter. There were cobwebs draped across the paint tins and a few woodlice scurrying across the cardboard under my feet, but other than that it hadn't changed at all. I lay down under the iron steps, immediately feeling the familiar way in which the cardboard underfoot snugly accommodated my body. Curled up in the shelter that had been my home, I felt comforted, as if somehow the tomcat was there with me. I wrapped my paws in front of my face and went to sleep.

The café remained closed for several days for refurbishment. Once the walls were finished, Debbie attacked the woodwork, sanding and smoothing, before repainting the sills and window frames with white gloss paint. Midweek, a large van pulled up outside to deliver the new serving counter. The installation was a noisy process, which I was happy to avoid, staying in the flat for the duration of the drilling and banging. Only when everything had gone quiet in the café and the van had driven away did I pad downstairs to investigate.

When Debbie saw me on the bottom step she smiled. 'Aha, here she is!'

I lifted my tail in greeting and walked over to her. She and Sophie were behind the new counter, stacking napkins and cutlery in drawers. It was much less cumbersome than the one it had replaced, with a solid wooden top and whitewashed panelling on the front. Every now and then Debbie stroked its knotted surface approvingly.

I moved across the floor, taking in the other alterations to the café. The room that had once been a study in grey was now vibrant with colour. Debbie had placed gingham cushions on the seats and candy-striped oil-cloths on the tabletops. Pictures framed in driftwood and heart-shaped wreaths of rosebuds were hanging on the pink walls. A jug of tulips stood on the mantelpiece over the stove, alongside a blackboard upon which Debbie had neatly chalked the menu. The café was inviting and homely, almost unrecognizable from its previous drab incarnation. I felt irrationally proud of the trail of pink paw prints that weaved across the floor as if they represented my own contribution to the makeover.

Padding from the counter towards the window, I was momentarily alarmed when I noticed that my shoebox had gone from the sill. As if reading my mind, Debbie said, 'Don't worry, Molly, I haven't thrown it away – it's here, look.' She pointed to a nook inside the fireplace, a low stone shelf in the side-wall next to the stove, where my shoebox had been tucked. 'I thought it might look better somewhere less prominent,' Debbie explained, apologetically. 'I've put a cushion for you on the windowsill instead.'

I jumped up and stepped onto the pink gingham cushion, turning in circles to feel its texture and firmness. Debbie smiled as she watched me from behind the counter, with Sophie on a stool beside her, folding menu cards. The cushion felt good, and I started to knead it appreciatively with my front paws.

'Glad you like the cushion, Molls. Now check this out . . .' Debbie took one of the menus from Sophie's neat pile. 'We've got a new name too. Molly's Café. It was Sophie's idea, wasn't it, Soph?'

I looked up. Debbie was walking towards me, beaming as she held the menu in front of me.

'Well, it makes sense. She acts like she's the boss already,' Sophie said drily from behind the counter.

I felt quite overcome by emotion. I didn't know whether I was more touched by the fact that Debbie had named the café after me or that it was Sophie who had suggested it. I did know, however, that I loved the name as much as I loved the new café, and that it was now, without a doubt, my home.

22

Molly's Café opened for business the following day. I could sense Debbie's nerves as she turned the door sign to 'Open', then stood behind the counter, watching anxiously as people walked passed the window. It was a Thursday, which was market day in Stourton, and the streets were busy, yet the café remained empty, overlooked by the passers-by intent on visiting the market. I sat on my cushion in the window, willing for it to rain so that people would be driven indoors, but the sky stayed stubbornly blue.

At lunchtime the bell over the door tinkled at last, and a couple with a small child walked in. The little girl immediately set off to follow the pink paw prints on the floor, tottering excitedly to the end of the trail, where she found me sitting majestically on my cushion. 'Cat!' she exclaimed, pointing at me and clapping her hands, to her parents' indulgent laughter.

Debbie brought a high chair out of the kitchen, and the family ate lunch at the table in the window while I washed on my cushion next to them. Debbie cast nervous glances in our direction when the little girl staggered towards me and grabbed a handful of my fur, but I merely twitched my tail while her mother gently loosened her grip.

'Can I tempt any of you with a pudding?' Debbie offered as she cleared away their plates, gesturing to the selection of cakes and pastries on the serving counter. She beamed as the family ordered two chocolate brownies and an ice cream.

The sight of customers at the front table seemed to have an encouraging effect on passers-by, drawing them to the window to read the menu and peer inside. By mid-afternoon the market had started to wind down and there was a steady trickle through the door of weary shoppers, longing for a restorative slice of cake after the exertion of market-shopping. They spoke in hushed voices, but I could detect appreciative murmurings as they admired the café's decor and perused the new menu. Relieved of their heavy bags, they soon began to relax in the calm surroundings of the café, soothed by my purring presence as I weaved between the tables. By late afternoon I was feeling sleepy and soon dozed off in the window, to the pleasant background hum of small talk and laughter.

Jo came around after work the following day, bringing the usual Friday night takeaway. 'I *love* what you've done with the place, Debs!' she said sincerely. 'And I particularly love the colour on the walls. *So* much nicer than those drab greys you were considering.'

'Yes, you were right, Jo – you can stop going on about it now,' Debbie replied, emptying the dishwasher for the second time that evening.

Jo dished the food onto plates while Debbie finished up in the kitchen.

'So, how's it going? Has the redesign paid off?' Jo asked, as soon as they had tucked into their meal.

'So far, so good. We had twelve covers at lunch today, and then eight more for tea,' Debbie announced proudly.

'This is a turning point for you, Debs – I can feel it,' Jo replied.

'I really hope you're right, Jo. I can't afford for it to fail. I'm in debt up to here,' Debbie held her hand up to her chin, 'and I've yet to replace the boiler.'

Jo nodded slowly, glancing sidelong at Debbie as she took a sip of wine. 'So, has John been in to see the new look?' she asked casually.

Debbie bristled. 'No, why would he?'

'I just thought he might have popped in to, you know, sample the wares.' Debbie shot her a look. 'I mean the food, obviously!' Jo laughed.

'Well, he did text me earlier in the week,' Debbie admitted.

Jo looked at her shrewdly. 'Go on.'

'He said something about going for a drink, but I was too busy to reply and then it kind of slipped my mind.' Debbie's tone was offhand.

Jo stared at her. 'It slipped your mind?' she repeated incredulously.

'Oh, Jo, don't be like that. He probably just wanted to nag me about the boiler.'

'Of course,' Jo agreed sarcastically. 'I'm sure he asks all his customers for a drink, just to remind them to replace their boilers.'

Debbie rolled her eyes. 'Please, Jo, just leave it, would you?'

There was an awkward pause between them while Jo sipped her wine and Debbie played with the food on her plate. Jo finally broke the silence. 'Well, all I'm saying is that he's a nice bloke, and there's a lot to be said for that. Plus, he's not a member of the Lawn Bowls Society, and there's a lot to be said for that too.' Jo drew her finger and thumb across her lips to indicate that she would say no more on the matter, then went to the kitchen to find another bottle of wine.

When she returned to the table, Debbie sighed and put her fork down on her plate. 'You're right, Jo, he does seem like a very nice bloke. But I've been there before, haven't I? My ex seemed like a nice bloke, and look how that ended up.'

Jo conceded that Debbie had a point. 'But how can you know, unless you give him a chance?' she asked softly.

'I can't risk any more disruption for Sophie,' Debbie answered firmly, her eyes starting to well up. 'For the first time in – I don't know how long – she's actually talking to me rather than shouting at me. She needs some stability in her life right now, and if that means me putting my love life on hold, then so be it.'

I pondered Debbie's words later that evening as I settled down on her bed for the night. Her discomfort, when asked about John, had been obvious, and she could not change the subject fast enough. Like Jo, I was baffled by Debbie's dismissal of his interest, and by her apparent unwillingness to give him a chance.

Perhaps Debbie was right that introducing John into the family dynamic might upset Sophie. I had also noticed the change in Sophie's attitude of late, and it wasn't just in the way she treated me. She seemed calmer, more settled and less angry. She was making more of an effort to confine her mess to her bedroom; I no longer had to pick my way through the debris of her school books and discarded shoes to find space on the sofa for a nap. I also couldn't remember the last time I had been woken by a door slamming, or been called a 'mangy fleabag', and she and Debbie hadn't argued for weeks. Whatever accounted for the change in Sophie's attitude, I shared Debbie's relief and, like her, I hoped it would last. If Debbie thought that going out for a drink with John might jeopardize the new equilibrium, then I felt duty-bound to believe her.

With the arrival of spring, Stourton started to come to life. Tourists and day-trippers milled around the streets, looking for ways to spend their money in the picturesque country town. Market day was always busy in the café, but even on non-market days a continuous stream of customers came through the door from about eleven in the morning. After a week of begging Sophie to help out after school and at weekends, Debbie finally admitted that she was going to have to take on some help, and a young waitress was hired.

The increased custom left Debbie exhausted, and had a tiring effect on me as well. I found I was napping for increasingly long periods, either on my cushion in the window or, on particularly warm days when the windowsill overheated, inside my shoebox in the fireplace. When I needed to stretch my legs I would prowl around the café, slipping between chair legs on the lookout for stray tuna flakes or cake crumbs.

Customers often asked Debbie about me, and she relished telling the story of how she had found me in the alley and decided to name the café after me. 'Don't let her fool you into thinking she's hungry, though,' Debbie warned them, wagging a finger at me as I eyed their sandwiches or clotted-cream-covered scones. 'She's getting a bit greedy, this one. It'll be time for a diet soon!' The diners laughed as I flicked my tail, before padding haughtily back to my cushion.

One Saturday night Sophie and Debbie were chatting in the café after closing time. I had been lying in the shoebox trying to sleep, but my back felt stiff and I could not settle. Thinking that stretching my legs might help, I jumped down and set off on a circuit around the café, idly looking for crumbs under the tables. Sophie had sat down at the serving counter, chatting through the kitchen doorway to Debbie. I noticed Sophie watching me as I made my way awkwardly between the tables.

'Mum, the cat's walking a bit funny,' she said, a note of concern in her voice.

'What do you mean, she's walking funny?' Debbie called back. She poked her head through the door and glanced at me, with soapy rubber gloves on her hands. 'She looks fine to me, Soph,' she said, before returning to the sink. The stiffness in my back was becoming more pronounced, compounded by a dull ache that, no matter how I stretched, I couldn't shift.

I made my way over to the window and, with more

effort than normal, jumped up onto the cushion. I started to wash, beginning with a gentle wipe of my face and paws, but when I turned my head to lick my shoulder blades I was seized by a sudden sharp pain in my abdomen. I let out an involuntarily yelp, and out of the corner of my eye I saw Sophie lift her head to look at me. The sudden pain was followed by a pressure in my belly, and no matter how I twisted on the cushion, I could not find a position that relieved it. I flopped onto my side and slowed my breathing to try and ease my discomfort.

Sophie stood up from her stool and began to walk towards me. 'Molly, are you okay?' she asked nervously.

There was a tightening sensation in my belly and, though I was touched by Sophie's concern, I couldn't summon the faculties to respond to her. The pressure in my abdomen was intensifying, and I felt like I was about to burst. Just as Sophie reached the windowsill, the pressure became so overwhelming that I had no choice but to give in to my urge to push.

I heard Sophie scream. 'Mum!' she shouted. 'Come here, *quick!* Molly's just . . . exploded!'

Debbie rushed into the café from the kitchen, still wearing her yellow rubber gloves. She ran to the windowsill and looked down at me. 'Oh, my God,' she exclaimed, her face aghast. 'She hasn't exploded, Sophie, she's giving birth!'

23

I lay on my side with my eyes closed, my head spinning. I could feel a dampness spreading across the cushion underneath me, but all I cared about was that the intense pressure in my abdomen had eased. I half-opened my eyes and saw Debbie and Sophie staring at me with identical shocked expressions on their faces.

Sophie clapped her hand over her mouth. 'Urgh, I think I'm going to be sick. That's disgusting,' she said.

Debbie turned to her sharply. 'It's not disgusting, Sophie – it's childbirth, and it's the most beautiful thing that can happen to a woman.'

Sophie stared back at her, open-mouthed. 'Mum, Molly's not a woman, she's a cat!'

Debbie frowned as she started to peel the rubber gloves off her hands. 'Of course she's a cat, Soph. Now stop gawping and get a towel, please.'

Sophie ran into the kitchen and I could hear her rummaging inside a cupboard.

Meanwhile Debbie knelt down on the floor next to the windowsill and stroked me on the head. 'You saucy minx, Molly. How did you find time for that, eh?' she chided me softly.

I started to purr. The initial shock of what had happened was passing and, for now at least, I wasn't in pain. I lifted my head from the cushion and turned to look at the tiny ball of damp fur – my kitten – that was nestling between my hind legs. It was squirming helplessly, so I propped myself up on my forelegs and began to give it a thorough, invigorating wash.

Sophie ran across the café and handed a towel to Debbie. They both watched in silence as I cleaned the kitten from head to tail. Sophie made a gagging sound as I chewed through the cord that still connected the kitten to my body, but Debbie elbowed her firmly in the ribs and told her to 'Shh!'

When I felt the pressure start to build in my abdomen again, I flopped back onto the cushion, knowing there was nothing I could do to fight the pain that would soon follow. While I waited for the urge to push to seize me, Debbie carefully took the first kitten and wrapped it in the towel, giving it a gentle rub all over and checking inside its mouth, before placing it close to my body.

'A tabby, Molls, just like you,' she whispered. Debbie and Sophie were kneeling on the floor next to the windowsill, their faces an equal mix of worry and excitement. I purred at them and Debbie reached out a hand and stroked my head. 'Keep it up, Molly, you're doing brilliantly,' she encouraged. I started to mew as the tightening sensation in my belly started to spread. I felt as if I was being gripped from the inside, and my limbs became rigid. 'Push the pain away, Molly – that's what the midwife told me,' Debbie said. And so I did.

As with the first kitten, the pain stopped the moment the second one arrived. I allowed myself a few breaths before tending to it, cleaning it quickly and efficiently. Although I knew there were more to come, my body seemed to be allowing me a temporary reprieve, and I was able to lie down and recover while my two kittens burrowed deep into my fur to feed.

'Shall I put the kettle on?' Sophie asked, looking suddenly drained.

Debbie agreed that tea was an excellent idea. While Sophie was in the kitchen, Debbie pulled two chairs up to the windowsill and lowered the blind in the window. The dusk had turned to darkness outside and the café interior was visible from the street. 'There you go, Molly,' she said softly. 'A little privacy might help.'

Sophie returned with two mugs of tea and they sat down on their chairs to wait.

'It brings it all back, you know,' Debbie said wistfully.

Sophie grimaced in a way that implied she'd heard it all before. 'At least you only had to push one out, Mum. Who knows how many Molly's got in there!'

Debbie laughed. 'That's true, Soph. Although you were so slow to come out – I probably could have delivered a whole litter in the time you took.'

Sophie winced. 'Urgh, Mum, please can we stop talking about this?'

'Okay,' Debbie said, taking a sip of her tea. 'Nineteen hours, that's all I'm saying. Nineteen hours. Of pain.' She smiled into her tea as Sophie rolled her eyes.

'Oh, all right, Mum. I didn't do it on purpose, you know.' Sophie was beginning to look riled. 'And besides, didn't you just say childbirth was the greatest thing that could happen to a woman?'

'I know, love, I'm only teasing,' Debbie laughed, placing a hand on her daughter's knee. 'And yes, it was the greatest thing that ever happened to me. *You* were the greatest thing that ever happened to me. You still are.'

Without taking her eyes off me, Debbie took Sophie's hand and gave it a squeeze. Sophie pulled a face, but they stayed that way, hand-in-hand, watching as I lay listlessly on the cushion. Before long I began to twist and squirm in pain once more.

'Oh, here we go,' Debbie said excitedly, putting her mug on the table and leaning forward in her chair. The third kitten emerged swiftly. I washed it and then Debbie rubbed it briskly with a towel and checked it over. 'We're like a well-oiled machine now, aren't we, girls?' Debbie joked, as she placed number three next to its siblings. There was no time to linger, however, as I was seized almost immediately by the urge to push again, and soon kitten number four had arrived. 'Look at that,' Debbie said, when all four were lying in a row, suckling happily. 'Four matching tabbies. How are we going to tell them apart, Molls?'

I wanted to purr, but could not muster the energy. Delivering the last two in such quick succession had left me exhausted, as if all the strength had been sucked from me. I could feel tiredness like I had never known creeping over me, so I lowered my head onto the cushion and closed my eyes.

'I think she's gone to sleep, Mum. Do you think that's all of them?' Sophie whispered.

'I don't know,' Debbie replied. I felt her hand lightly press my abdomen. 'Oh, hang on,' and she pressed more firmly. 'Sorry, girls, it's not time for sleep yet. There's another one in there!'

I knew that Debbie was right, but the tiredness

was so overwhelming that I was powerless to fight it. When I felt the familiar tightening in my belly I had no strength to respond.

'Come on, girl – you know the drill. Push the pain away,' Debbie urged, but I was too weak to lift my head, let alone push another kitten out.

I let out a long yowl of pain as a searing sensation pierced me from the inside. My body convulsed with an agony that seemed to fill my entire being, from my nose to the tip of my tail. I felt like I was being consumed from within and could do nothing except succumb helplessly. I collapsed, breathless, my head lolling over the cushion's edge.

'Mum, what's wrong, why is she just lying there?' I heard Sophie ask nervously.

'Come on, girl, you're nearly there.' Debbie was rubbing my cheek in an effort to wake me up.

'She's gone to sleep, look!' Sophie lifted one of my eyelids, but my eye had rolled up into my head as I began to drift out of consciousness. 'How will we get the kitten out, if she won't push?'

I didn't hear Debbie's response. Everything fell silent as I gratefully sank into a blissful blackness. I don't know how long I remained that way, but the next thing I knew I was jolted awake by a searing pain. Debbie was on the floor by the windowsill, her face close to mine.

'Come on, Molly, you can do it!' Her voice was loud and commanding.

Pain pulled and tugged at every fibre of my being, and I wanted nothing more than to fall back into the delicious darkness of sleep. But Debbie seemed determined not to let me, rubbing me between the ears every time I closed my eyes. Buoyed up by her dedication, I summoned the energy for one final push. In my exhausted state it took longer than before, and I was aware of Debbie and Sophie holding their breath as I bore down one last time.

They both gasped as my fifth kitten emerged. I collapsed back onto the cushion and panted for a few moments, ecstatic relief mixed with exhaustion flooding through me. I was too weak to prop myself up, so Debbie tended to the kitten, then held it in front of my face for me to see. 'A bit of a bruiser, this one. Must have smarted a bit. Good on you, girl!' she said in admiration. I looked at the kitten. He was twice the size of the others and, unlike his siblings, jet-black with a white blob on his chest. Just like his dad, I thought with a smile.

Before long all five kittens were feeding contentedly. Debbie ran upstairs to find a bottle of champagne, surprising Sophie by giving her a small serving of her own. They clinked glasses but, before taking a sip,

Debbie shouted, 'Hang on a minute, we mustn't forget the proud mummy!'

A couple of minutes later she placed a saucer of cream on the windowsill next to me. I purred my appreciation but, before I could even take a lick, I fell fast asleep.

24

The following morning Debbie carried me, and my five sleeping kittens, upstairs to the flat. She placed our cushion carefully inside a wide cardboard box next to the living-room fireplace. 'There you go, Molls,' she said when I lifted my head drowsily to look around. 'I thought you might want a bit of peace and quiet.'

The next few days passed in a haze of contented exhaustion. Debbie and Sophie came and went, eating at the table, watching TV, chatting on the sofa, but their lives receded into a background blur to which I was largely oblivious. I was perpetually tending to the kittens, seemingly feeding or cleaning one of them at all times. Day and night had little meaning for me; I slept whenever the kittens slept, regardless of whether the room was lit by sunshine or moonlight. I occasionally clambered out of the box to eat from the dish that Debbie had placed nearby, but other than that I remained inside our cardboard fortress, interested only in the immediate concerns of my offspring.

Debbie periodically came upstairs to check on us. She tiptoed over and peered inside the box, beaming when she found all five kittens blissfully kneading me while they fed. 'Aw, look at them, Molly. Aren't they gorgeous?' she clucked, and I basked sleepily in her admiration.

'What are you going to call them?' I heard Jo's voice say one evening. She had come up to the flat, to see the kittens for the first time.

'Goodness, I haven't even thought about names yet,' Debbie replied. 'I'm going to have to learn to tell them apart first!'

The kittens were about ten days old. Their blue eyes were beginning to open and they emitted helpless high-pitched squeaks whenever they were picked up.

'This one's my favourite,' said Jo indulgently, lifting one of the tiny tabbies in the palm of her hand. 'Look at that adorable splodge of white on her pink nose. I could just eat you up!' she said tenderly to the mewling kitten.

I lay in my box, vicariously enjoying the praise being lavished on my brood.

'Yes, she is a cutie, isn't she?' Debbie agreed. 'Well, I think she's a she. Of course we can't be sure just yet.'

'She looks like a Purdy to me,' Jo said, grinning sideways at Debbie.

'Purdy,' Debbie repeated thoughtfully, taking the kitten from Jo's hands and examining it closely. 'Yes, I can see that,' she agreed, and Jo clapped her hands like an excited child. 'Purdy pink-nose,' Debbie said.

'With a white splodge,' Jo added.

'Yes, that might help me to recognize her,' Debbie said seriously.

Having decided on a name for one kitten, Debbie felt obliged to do the same for the rest of the litter, and she and Sophie spent an evening on the living-room floor studying them closely, looking for inspiration in their markings and nascent personalities.

'I think this little one's a Maisie,' Debbie said about the smallest tabby, who was already showing signs of being the shyest of the five. 'And this big brute of a thing,' she said, picking up the squirming jet-black boy, 'needs a proper boy's name.'

Unable to come to any agreement, Sophie moved to the sofa to consult cat-naming websites on her phone. As the evening wore on, they dismissed countless names with increasing alacrity.

'Jeffrey? You can't call a cat Jeffrey!' Sophie jeered, as Debbie held the black kitten aloft.

'I think it sounds very distinguished,' Debbie said defensively.

'Mum, it's a middle-aged accountant's name. You can't do that to him!'

It was a long evening, but Debbie would not go to bed until they had agreed on names for the whole litter. Eventually, with the help of Sophie's phone, they had reached a consensus on names for all five. Debbie knelt down next to the cardboard box and pointed to each kitten in turn.

'Tabby-with-white-splodge: Purdy. Tabby-without-white-splodge: Bella. Tabby-with-white-tail-tip: Abby. Shy-tabby: Maisie. Black-and-white-boy: Eddie. Agreed?'

Sophie nodded wearily.

'Phew, thanks goodness for that,' Debbie said, holding her hand up to high-five Sophie. 'We can go to bed now.'

By the time they entered their fourth week the kittens were becoming more sociable, beginning to clamber out of the cardboard box and explore the room beyond. I revelled in their proud exhibitionism, loving the way they egged each other on into acts of increasingly acrobatic dexterity. They played energetically for hours, before falling suddenly asleep mid-game, huddled together on the rug or sofa cushion.

I had begun to leave them alone for short periods, allowing myself brief trips downstairs to the café and the street outside. Spring was in full swing: the air smelt heady with pollen, and songbirds were busy tending to their young in the trees. I never stayed out for long, knowing that the kittens became distressed if they noticed my absence. Nevertheless I savoured the brief moments I had to myself, appreciating every second of my rediscovered independence.

Some of the café's regular customers, noticing that I no longer slept in the window, had asked after me. Debbie explained that I was on 'maternity leave' from the café and had moved upstairs to the flat for the time being. Whenever I appeared at the bottom of the stairs, customers would turn and look, keen to give me a stroke and congratulate me on motherhood. I lapped up their attention, grateful that for once I was being fussed over, rather than the kittens.

One Saturday morning I was lying in the cardboard box feeding the kittens while Debbie and Sophie ate breakfast. Debbie tore open a letter as she sipped her tea. 'Oh, my God.' She placed her hand over her mouth in shock.

'What is it?' Sophie asked, alarmed. Debbie's hand was shaking as she reread the contents of the letter. 'Mum, tell me!' Sophie insisted.

'It's from the Environmental Health,' Debbie replied. 'Someone has reported the café for a breach of health-and-safety – for having a cat on the premises.' Her face had gone pale and her lip was starting to tremble. '"The café licence clearly states that no animals are to be allowed on the premises,"' she read. '"Breach of this regulation will result in the immediate closure of the business on hygiene grounds."'

She and Sophie stared at each other across the table in silence.

'Oh, my God, Soph, what are we going to do?' Debbie asked, her voice wavering. She looked over at the kittens, who had finished their feed and were scrambling out of the cardboard box, ready to play. 'If they could close us down for having one cat, what will they do when they find out there are six!' she said, pressing the palm of her hand against her cheek.

Sophie took the letter from her mum to read it herself. 'Look, don't panic, Mum. It's just talking about the café. It doesn't say anything about the flat. As long as we keep them up here, we're not in breach of anything.'

'Keep them up here?' Debbie laughed mirthlessly. 'That's fine for a few more weeks, but look at them, Soph – they're on the move already. This flat's hardly big enough for you, me and Molly, as it is. Let alone with six of them! And Molly needs to go outside – it's cruel to keep her cooped up in here.' Debbie looked like she was about to burst into tears.

Sophie stood up and put an arm around her mother's shoulder in a show of support. 'Oh, Mum, it'll be all right. We'll find a way round it,' she soothed.

'It's just so typical, Soph. Just as things were starting to go right, for a change.' Debbie started to sob, impervious to Sophie's attempts to reassure her.

I climbed out of the box and walked over to Debbie, partly because I felt she needed me, but also because I needed reassurance myself. Debbie's reaction to the letter was ominous, and I was frightened to think what it might mean for me and my kittens.

Debbie lifted me carefully onto her lap and held my face between her hands. 'Oh, Molly,' she said sadly.

I looked into her tear-filled eyes, waiting for her to tell me that things weren't as bad as she feared and that everything would be okay, but she didn't say a word. As I watched the fat tears roll down her cheeks, I felt the first pangs of alarm that my happy life in the café might be about to come to an end.

25

'But who would have reported us? All the customers love Molly.' Debbie's toast lay uneaten on her plate as the letter's meaning began to sink in.

She stood up and began to pace across the room, clutching the letter in her hand. Eddie crouched on the rug, wiggling his bottom from side to side as he prepared to pounce on her feet. Oblivious to his presence Debbie dropped onto the sofa, her face a picture of consternation. Within seconds, Eddie had scampered across the rug and started to climb up her trouser leg.

'I think I can guess who did it,' Sophie said glumly.

Debbie looked up, confused.

'There's an old lady who walks past the café every day,' Sophie continued, sitting down on the sofa next to Debbie. 'Dyed hair, face like she's sucking a lemon.'

'With the shopping trolley?' Debbie interjected. Sophie nodded. 'I know the one.' A puzzled frown was beginning to form on Debbie's brow. 'But she's never said a word to me. What's the café to her?'

'Well, she has spoken to me. Lots of times,' Sophie replied, lowering her eyes.

Debbie stared at Sophie, confused. 'When? What's she said?'

'She's usually at the bus stop when I get back from school,' Sophie said quietly. 'At first she just gave me dirty looks, then she started muttering about how people like us are ruining the town – that we're not welcome here and never will be.'

'People like us?' Debbie repeated, the colour rising in her cheeks. 'What's that supposed to mean?' Sophie shrugged. Debbie's face was flushed with anger and indignation. She looked like she was about to speak, but she bit her lip and told Sophie to carry on.

'It just kind of grew from there. Every time she passed she would make some comment, usually about you. Stupid stuff, like "She'll run that business into the ground" or "No one in their right mind would eat food that she's prepared." I just ignored her, I thought she was crazy.'

Debbie's mouth fell open. 'What the . . . ? How dare she, the miserable old—' She stopped in mid-sentence as a thought struck her. 'But, Sophie, why haven't you told me any of this before?'

Sophie looked down, avoiding her mother's gaze.

Purdy had crawled onto her lap and was washing herself proudly, showing off the grooming techniques that I had taught her.

'I figured she was just a mad old woman. And I didn't want to worry you, Mum. You were so down about the business already. I thought it would be the last straw.'

'So you kept it to yourself? Oh, Soph, you shouldn't have done that.' Debbie's eyes were brimming with tears, and when I looked across at Sophie, I noticed that hers were the same.

'I was really scared, Mum. You kept saying how the café was your new start, and I knew you were worried about the locals not accepting you. I thought if you knew what she was saying, you'd decide to have another fresh start somewhere else.'

'Oh, Soph, I would never do that,' Debbie protested.

'But you'd already done it once, Mum. You made the decision to come here, didn't you? You took me out of school, made me leave all my friends. I never asked to come here, did I? How was I to know you wouldn't do the same thing again?'

Debbie's head dropped and I saw tears falling onto Eddie, who was rolling in her lap, batting the tassels on the hem of her jumper. Debbie wiped her eyes and turned to face Sophie. 'I promise you, Soph, I will never make a decision like that again without talking to you first. And I'm so sorry you've been dealing with all of this on your own. I should have known something was going on.' She put her hand on Sophie's leg, where it was immediately pounced on by Purdy.

Sophie nodded and smiled tearfully, gently trying to prise Purdy off her mother's hand. Purdy immediately twisted round to attack Sophie's fingers, biting her thumb as ferociously as she could with her tiny teeth. 'I don't know why, Mum, but for some reason that woman's had it in for you from the start. I guess seeing Molly in the window just gave her the excuse she needed.'

By now, all five kittens had joined Debbie and Sophie on the sofa. Bella and Abby were walking along the cushions behind them, their tails veering from side to side as they tried to maintain their balance; Purdy and Eddie were playing on Sophie and Debbie's laps, and Maisie was washing on the sofa arm by Debbie's elbow.

'And now look at us!' Debbie said, wiping her eyes and gesturing towards the kittens surrounding them. 'The old battleaxe would have a field day. She thought one cat was bad. What would she do if she knew there were six?'

Sophie laughed and stroked Purdy, who, worn out by playing, had curled up in a tight ball next to her leg.

'But seriously, Mum, what are we going to do with them? Can we really keep them all in the flat?'

Hidden inside the cardboard box, I pricked up my ears.

'For now we don't have any other choice,' Debbie answered. 'The kittens aren't even a month old yet – they're too young to be separated from Molly. But beyond that . . . I'm not sure, Soph. It's a small flat, and Molly's not used to being solely an indoor cat. We'll have to think of what's best for her.'

Debbie's response worried me. She had sidestepped the question and there was something in her tone that suggested resignation. The only certainty I could take from her words was that, as long as the kittens were dependent on me, we would remain in the flat. It wasn't much comfort, but it was all I had.

The next time I stepped into the hall, I discovered that a large piece of plyboard had been placed across the top of the stairs, blocking my access to the café. Although I understood that Debbie had no alternative, I felt my throat constrict every time I looked at it. It was a stark reminder that I was now confined upstairs and, in effect, a prisoner in the flat.

Gazing at the skyline from the living-room window was a poor substitute for being able to come and go as I pleased. My loss of liberty was largely symbolic –

since the kittens were born I had chosen to spend most of my waking hours with them in the flat – but I bitterly missed my short forays into the café and the outside world. They had been fleeting moments of independence for me, when I was – however briefly – free from the responsibilities of motherhood. Meeting customers in the café, or being out in the fresh air, reminded me that life outside the flat continued, and that I still had an identity beyond being a mother to my kittens.

Knowing there was nothing I could do about my confinement, I devoted all my energy and attention to the kittens. They were becoming more adventurous and sociable by the day, and I was constantly surprised by their physical and emotional development. Although Eddie had remained significantly larger than the others, he had a gentle, diffident nature and was easily cowed into submission by his sisters. Maisie was the most nervous of the five, springing into the air with her tail fluffed at any sudden noise or movement. Bella and Abby were a tight duo, always play-fighting together, and Purdy was by far the most mischievous and extroverted of the litter. She was always the first to explore new parts of the flat, prising open doors with her paw while the others watched intently from the sidelines.

Watching my kittens grow was a bittersweet experience. I found them endlessly fascinating and longed to see what changes their development would bring next. But with those changes came the certainty that, eventually, they would no longer be dependent on me. When that time came, I knew Debbie would have to decide what was going to happen to us. I tried to put thoughts of the future out of my mind but, when the kittens were asleep, I couldn't help but wonder where they would end up and what my future would hold when they had gone.

While I had the kittens to look after, Debbie had other demands on her time. The café's growing popularity presented her with a fresh set of concerns, about staffing levels, suppliers and wage bills. Having borrowed money to pay for the refurbishment and take on new staff, the stakes were higher than ever, if the café didn't continue to thrive. Even when she was in the flat, Debbie was often preoccupied, attending to business matters on her laptop or making work calls on the phone.

It happened gradually and imperceptibly but, as time went on, I began to sense that Debbie and I were no longer as close we used to be. By the time she had finished dinner and dealt with the evening's administrative jobs, she was exhausted and ready for bed. She had stopped confiding in me, the way she used to, and I couldn't shake the feeling that she was hiding something from me, and that it was tied up with the future of the café. I could not be sure, but I suspected that the time might come when Debbie would have to choose between the café and me. Knowing that Sophie's well-being and security depended on the café being a success, I was in no doubt that, if Debbie was forced to make a decision, she would choose the café.

At night, when everyone was asleep, I would jump onto the living-room windowsill. The amber glow of the street light illuminated the alleyway below and, if I pressed my head against the glass, I could just make out the dustbin beneath the window. To see the alley and not be able to step out into it, however, increased my feeling of isolation. Staring at the dark alley, I resolved that – if the worst were to happen – I would be prepared. If and when the time came, I would return to the alleyway rather than allow myself to be rehomed by a stranger. Sometimes the thought would rise, unbidden, that I wished the tomcat would come back, that being homeless would be less frightening if I had him by my side. But I knew that indulging in such daydreams would lead only to disappointment and I dismissed them from my mind. I had survived as an alley-cat before; if necessary, I could do so again.

26

In the weeks that followed the bombshell of the council's letter, uncertainty about my future became a constant backdrop to my life. I was intensely conscious that every developmental leap in the kittens took them closer to independence, and me closer to possible homelessness. I lived in a limbo-like state. Sometimes I found the uncertainty unbearable, and I fantasized about running away. At least that would spare Debbie the pain of having to make the decision herself.

Debbie, meanwhile, was increasingly stressed about the café, which had started to lose customers. When she wasn't in the café she was at the dining table, going through the accounts or typing emails on her laptop. I couldn't help but notice that her relationship with Sophie was also deteriorating. Sensing that her mother was preoccupied, Sophie became sarcastic and stroppy.

I was reminded, unhappily, of how she had behaved when I first moved in.

It seemed like things were beginning to unravel for all of us, and the worst part was that I felt responsible. I could see that the presence of the kittens was adding to the pressures on Debbie. They were six weeks old now and were hungry, boisterous and playful. Their adventurousness was no longer confined to the living room: they got into the kitchen cupboards, underneath the beds, and on one occasion Purdy climbed up inside the chimney breast and had to be rescued by Debbie from the soot-filled flue. Much as I adored their liveliness, I bitterly regretted that it was always Debbie who had to step in when one of them needed rescuing, or to clean up their trail of mess and destruction. I could do nothing but stand back and watch and I worried that, much as Debbie loved the kittens, her patience was being stretched to breaking point.

One evening she had finally sat down with the laptop, having just finished washing up in the kitchen, when Sophie walked in, frowning. 'Mum, have you seen my geography project?' she asked sharply.

Debbie was squinting at the screen through her glasses. 'Mmm?' she replied, distractedly.

'Mum?' Sophie snapped. 'I left it on the kitchen worktop this morning. It's gone. Have you seen it?'

Debbie took off her glasses and turned to look at Sophie. 'Sorry, love, what did you say?'

'My geography project, Mum. It's due tomorrow. I left it on the worktop.' I could see that Sophie's frustration was about to turn to anger.

'Sorry, love, I don't remember seeing it,' Debbie replied. She put on her glasses and turned back to the laptop. 'I put the recycling out this afternoon,' she added vaguely.

'The recycling?'

'Yes, there was a stack of old newspapers in the kitchen . . .'

Sophie stared at her mother. 'A stack of old newspapers? And did you happen to notice whether my geography project was on the top of that stack?'

Debbie frowned and rubbed her forehead. 'Sorry, love, I don't recall seeing any project, but I'm not sure—'

Sophie had gone, slamming the living-room door behind her. I heard her run downstairs, and a few seconds later the café door slammed too.

Debbie dropped her head into her hands. She sighed deeply, then closed the laptop and stood up, walking across the room to the sofa. Her cheeks were pink and I knew that tears would soon follow. I had tried to keep some distance from the situation, not wanting to inflame matters between mother and daughter by getting involved, but I could not sit and watch Debbie cry. I climbed out of the cardboard box and went to sit by her ankles, looking up at her face.

Debbie noticed me and smiled tearfully. 'Oh, Molly,' she sighed, putting her hand down to stroke my ears.

That was all the invitation I needed. I jumped up onto her lap and rubbed my head against her damp cheek. I let her cry into my fur until the combination of her tears and my loose hairs sticking to her face meant that she had to reach for a tissue. When she had blown her nose, she held my face between her hands and looked me in the eye.

'Oh, Molly, what a mess I've made of things. What am I going to do, eh?' I blinked at her slowly, wanting to encourage Debbie to keep talking. There may have been nothing I could do to help, but I could listen. 'I don't know what to worry about more: that Sophie's starting to hate me again, or that the café's going under. So far I'm making a complete mess on both fronts.' She stroked my ears, and I rubbed my cheek along the side of her hand. 'You know the really crazy thing, Molly? It turns out that you were what the customers wanted all along, but I didn't realize until it was too late.'

I looked at her inquisitively, not following what she was saying. 'It's "Molly's Café", isn't it?' she said by way of explanation. 'Everyone used to see you in the window, and that's why they came in. They expected you to be inside. They all loved hearing about the kittens – couldn't wait to meet them – but now I've had to tell people that you won't be coming downstairs any more. And, well, they're just not coming through the door like they used to.' Her eyes filled with tears again. 'If I let you downstairs, that witch will have me shut down by Environmental Health, but if I keep you up here we'll lose all our customers and the café will probably go under. So I'm damned if I do, and damned if I don't, aren't I?'

My head was spinning. I had had no idea my presence meant so much to the customers, and I felt a momentary glow of pride that I had been the reason many of them had come at all. But, on the other hand, this discovery merely reinforced my conviction that I was to blame for Debbie's predicament.

While she had been talking, Eddie had woken up and had jumped onto the sofa, his tail happily aloft. He climbed onto Debbie's lap alongside me and rolled onto his back. I pressed his exposed tummy with my paw and he squirmed from side to side, pretending that my foot was a foe he must fight off. Debbie watched Eddie and her tear-stained face melted into a smile.

'See, Molly – we're the same, you and I. We're just trying to do what's best for our children, aren't we?'

I purred in agreement. Even though we were no

closer to a solution, I was grateful for Debbie's words. If nothing else, they made me feel that we were on the same side once more.

A little while later Sophie returned home. Debbie and I listened as she let herself into the café kitchen and climbed the stairs.

'Hi, Soph,' Debbie called quietly.

Sophie pushed open the living-room door. 'Sorry about earlier, Mum,' she said, her voice conciliatory.

'I'm sorry too,' Debbie answered, relief spreading across her face. 'I'm sure we can find your project – it should still be in the box.'

'Don't worry Mum, I already found it. It's fine, just a bit smelly from the bin.'

Debbie smiled. 'Phew. Hopefully they won't mark it down for smelliness.'

'I don't think they will,' Sophie agreed.

'I tell you what: shall I make us both a hot chocolate?' Debbie suggested, and Sophie nodded.

Debbie reappeared a few minutes later with mugs of hot chocolate topped with whipped cream and mini-marshmallows. Sophie's face lit up, and for a moment she looked like a little girl rather than a teenager. They sat on the sofa sipping their drinks, whilst trying to bat a persistent Eddie away from the whipped cream. Sophie eventually gave up and allowed him to lick a blob of cream from the tip of her finger, his rumbling purr filling the whole room.

'So here's the deal, Sophie,' Debbie said, suddenly serious. 'The way things stand, we're not taking enough to make the monthly repayments for the loan. If we default on the loan, we stand to lose everything – the café, the flat, the whole lot will be repossessed.' Debbie paused, and Sophie inhaled deeply. 'So, the way I see it,' Debbie continued, 'we have two choices. We either soldier on as we are, hoping that people get used to the idea of Molly's Café with no Molly, but possibly defaulting on the loan if they don't.' Sophie nodded slowly. 'Or,' Debbie went on, 'we sell up now, before we fall behind on the repayments. We could probably get enough from the sale to break even; maybe even have enough left to use as a deposit on a little flat some-where.' She paused, watching anxiously as Sophie mulled over the dilemma. 'Well, what do you think?' she asked.

Sophie's face was intently serious, and I was struck by how quickly she had switched from little-girl mode to grown-up. 'I think . . . it's too soon to give up. You've put so much into this place, Mum, and I know you can make it work.' She put her hand on her mother's knee encouragingly and Debbie eyes instantly welled up.

'I don't know, Soph. I wish I had your faith in me,' she replied, wiping her eyes with a tissue.

'But what's the alternative, Mum? If you sell up and take the money – hopefully buy another little flat somewhere else – then what? We'll just be back to square one.'

Debbie nodded. 'I know – you're right, but it just feels like a massive risk, and I don't know if it's fair to do that to you. You've got your GCSEs coming up. I should be helping you, not accidentally throwing away your coursework because I'm too busy poring over these bloody accounts!'

Sophie laughed. 'Don't worry about my coursework, Mum. I can handle that. You just need to put everything into making the café work. I know you can do it.'

Debbie nodded tearfully, and Sophie leant over to give her a hug, squashing the still-purring Eddie between them.

After they had finished their hot chocolates they both stood up, ready for bed. As Debbie turned out the light, Sophie said, 'If we do stay here, Mum, what are you going to do about Molly and the kittens?'

Debbie paused. 'I don't know, Soph, I just don't know.'

27

'We need to build our profile on social media, apparently,' Debbie announced one Sunday afternoon from behind the laptop. She and Sophie were sitting at the dining-room table, both hard at work.

'Right,' Sophie replied vaguely, not lifting her eyes from her schoolwork.

'I should be tweeting and updating our Instagram feed at least twenty times a day, according to this new-business forum I've joined.'

Sophie looked at Debbie, and raised an eyebrow sceptically. 'Mum, do you even know what Instagram is?'

'Well, no, but I'm prepared to learn! You can show me, can't you? You're an expert at all that stuff.'

'I s'pose. I can show you if you like, but I've got to finish my revision.'

Sophie returned to her work, flicking studiously through the pages of her textbook. Debbie started to chuckle, and Sophie's eyes flicked towards her, puzzled and slightly annoyed.

'What now, Mum?'

'Sorry, love, I was just thinking: who would have believed, six months ago, that I would be pestering you to use Instagram, and you would be telling me that you can't because you've got work to do? Who'd have thought it, eh? Or, as a tweeter-er might say: *hashtag*-never-saw-that-coming.' Debbie snorted at her own joke.

Sophie rolled her eyes. 'Oh, Mum. Please don't ever use the word *tweeter-er* again.'

'*Hashtag*-OK,' Debbie replied with a giggle.

Sophie dropped the textbook onto the table and glared at her mother. 'Or the word *hashtag*. Seriously, Mum, stop distracting me. I've got work to do.'

Although the café's future still hung in the balance, Debbie and Sophie's conversation helped to clear the air between them. Debbie seemed to have drawn strength from Sophie's conviction that she mustn't give up on the café without a fight. She became ruthlessly focused on trying to make the business a success, and her research on the laptop led her to try all sorts of initiatives. She introduced a customer loyalty card;

tried various promotional offers, such as free cup of tea with every slice of cake; and even touted the notion of building a website for the café. That project had faltered, however, when Debbie had innocently enquired, 'What's HTML, Soph?'

'Mum, sorry, but no. Just, no,' Sophie had replied firmly, and Debbie had muttered that maybe the website could go on the back burner for now.

In spite of Sophie's evident frustration with some of her mother's schemes, their bickering remained good-natured. There was an atmosphere of female solidarity in the flat, which extended to me, too. It seemed that Debbie, Sophie and I had all reached the same conclusion: there was no certainty about what the future held for any of us, so we just had to make the best of what we had in the present. It was a strange time, knowing that we could all be about to lose what little security we had, but I took comfort in the camaraderie that had developed between us. Whatever fate had in store, it felt as though we would face it together.

I did my bit for morale in the flat by raising my kittens to the best of my ability. I made sure they were spotlessly clean at all times and scrupulously attentive to their own personal hygiene. If they were too boisterous or their play became aggressive, I could be a firm disciplinarian, putting them in their place with a swipe of my paw. But I also encouraged their independence and adventurousness, knowing that in later life they might need resilience and courage to fall back on. I took some comfort in knowing that I had provided them with the skills they needed to give them the best possible chance in life.

When the kittens were about eight weeks old, Debbie was going through the accounts books on Sunday evening when Sophie rushed in, her face flushed with excitement.

'Mum, look at this.' The kittens sensed her heightened mood and emerged from their various hiding points around the room, keen as always to be at the heart of the action. Sophie held out her phone to Debbie, who was putting her glasses on to view the tiny screen. She looked confused.

'I don't understand, Soph – is it a funny cat video?'

Sophie tutted impatiently. 'No, it's not a cat video, Mum. It's a cat café.'

Debbie's face was blank. 'A cat café?'

'Yes, like a normal café, except that it's got cats. Customers come specifically to see the cats; and to eat, of course.'

Debbie took the phone from Sophie's hand. 'But I don't understand: how is that possible? How do they get around health-and-safety?'

'I don't know, but it must be possible – someone else has done it!'

Debbie stared intently at the screen.

'We should do the same, Mum. It's obvious! We can keep Molly and the kittens, and the customers will love it.'

Debbie started to smile uncertainly. 'But that isn't . . . We couldn't . . . Surely it can't be that straightforward?'

'It could be, Mum,' Sophie laughed. 'There's not just one of these places – they're popping up all over the world. Cat cafés are the in-thing right now, and in case you hadn't noticed,' Sophie gestured to the kittens, who had jumped onto the dining chairs and were now scaling the tabletop, 'we've got the cats and we've got the café, so we're practically there already!'

Debbie's face wore a look of half-excitement, half-consternation, but Sophie was not done yet.

'And I've been thinking, Mum. You can tweak the menu, you know? Cat-shaped cookies, cupcakes with whiskers – that sort of thing. The tourists will go crazy for it.'

Debbie laughed nervously. 'I don't know, Sophie. It sounds lovely, but . . . could it really work?'

'Well, there's only one way to find out,' Sophie answered decisively. 'You need to ring the council and ask.'

Her enthusiasm was infectious, and I could feel my stomach lurch with excitement. But, like Debbie, I couldn't let myself get carried away. A voice in my head urged caution. It all sounded too good to be true.

28

Debbie picked up the phone to call the council first thing on Monday morning.

'Yes, hello, I'd like to speak to the department that looks after cafés and food outlets. Yes, thank you, I'll hold . . . ' She tapped the handset and looked out of the window, waiting to be put through. 'Oh, yes, hello. This might sound like a bit of a strange enquiry, but I'd like to speak to someone about turning a café into a cat café. Yes, a *cat* café. No, not a café for cats – a café for people, with cats in it. Okay, yes, I can hold . . . '

As she was repeatedly put on hold and passed between departments, her initial enthusiasm gave way to frustration. She glanced at her watch and drummed her fingers on the table. No one she spoke to was sure to whom she actually needed to speak; the only thing they were sure of was that it wasn't them.

'Oh, yes, hello,' she repeated wearily, after being put on hold for the fourth time. 'I'm trying to find out who I need to speak to about opening a cat café. I was just wondering what it might involve . . . Right, I see. Okay, thank you.'

Debbie placed the phone back in its cradle and rolled her head from side to side. I was lying on the dining table next to the phone, hoping that my presence would offer moral support.

'Well, Molly, apparently we need to write a letter. Why it took the best part of an hour to establish that, I'm not entirely sure. But a letter must be written, so a letter I shall write. Although not until I have had a cup of coffee.'

That evening Jo popped in for a chat and a play with the kittens. 'So how did you get on with the council this morning?' she asked, lifting Purdy out of the cardboard box for a cuddle.

Debbie threw her head back in despair. 'Well, apart from the fact that no one at the council has ever heard of a cat café, and they aren't sure which department would be responsible for one, plus they don't know what licences would be required, or what the hygiene regulations might be, or whether animal-welfare organizations need to be consulted . . . Apart from all of that, the answer to your question is: I got on great!'

Jo grimaced, before burying her face in Purdy's fur to blow a raspberry on her back.

At dinner that evening Debbie relayed her experience with the council to Sophie, and broke the news that the cat-café idea still seemed a long way off. Sophie looked annoyed and opened her mouth to speak, but Debbie cut her off. 'I know what you're going to say, Soph – don't give up. And I'm not giving up, I just wanted to warn you that this isn't going to be a quick or easy process, and we can't assume that we're going to get the answer we want from the council.'

Sophie's shoulders dropped and she sighed. 'Well done, Mum. I'm sure you're doing everything you can.'

That night I was woken by a strange sound. I lifted my head inside the cardboard box, my ears flicking as I tried to detect the source of the noise. I padded out of the living room, my senses on high alert. I could hear gurgling noises from the radiator pipes in the hall, but I could also detect a faint hissing coming from the café. I stood at the top of the stairs, my tail twitching. I knew that I risked Debbie's anger if she discovered me creeping downstairs under cover of night, but my instincts were telling me something was amiss. In the end it was the thought of my kittens sleeping in the next room that made up my mind: something was wrong, and it was my duty to investigate.

I launched myself at the plyboard panel, scrabbling over the top and knocking it backwards as I dropped onto the stairs. I slipped down the staircase, pausing on the bottom step to take in the sight of the café, which I had not seen since the night I gave birth. I felt a pang of longing when I noticed that my gingham cushion was still in place on the windowsill, as if waiting for my return. I hoped its presence was a sign that Debbie believed I would, one day, be allowed back in the café.

The hissing sound was coming from the kitchen, so I crept past the serving counter through the doorway. Instantly my fur prickled in alarm. The air smelt strangely sweet and thick. It made my nose tingle, and after a few breaths my head started to swim. I followed the sound of hissing to the boiler, which was emitting creaking metallic noises. There was water trickling down the wall behind it, a steady stream that was already forming a pool on the kitchen floor and was spreading out across the tiles.

I turned and made my way quickly out of the kitchen and upstairs to the flat. I paused to take some deep breaths of clean air in the hallway, before running up the second flight of stairs to Debbie's bedroom. Debbie was fast asleep and did not stir when I jumped onto the quilt beside her, or when I walked alongside her body and stood next to her face. I lifted one paw and tapped her lightly on the cheek. Her nose wrinkled and she lifted her hand, as if swatting a fly away, but her eyes remained closed. I patted her again, more insistently. This time she opened her eyes, startled to find me looming in front of her face. 'Oh, Molly, it's you,' she murmured sleepily.

I meowed, trying to convey the urgency of the situation.

'Shh, girl,' she said, lifting her hand sleepily to stroke my back. I meowed again, louder this time, and patted her cheek for a third time. 'Molly, I'm sleeping – leave me alone,' she protested. She closed her eyes and rolled away from me, pulling her pillow over her head.

In desperation, I jumped from the bed onto her dressing table which was crowded with plastic bottles and pots of make-up and old lipsticks. It was hard to find space for my feet among the cotton-wool pads and hairbrushes. After all the weeks I had spent chastising my kittens for destructive behaviour, I was aware of the irony of my current predicament. I felt guilty even contemplating it, but I knew what I had to do: I closed my eyes and took a deep breath, then swiped firmly across the contents of the dressing table with my paw.

Immediately there was a loud clattering, as the first bottle toppled over and knocked those around it, which in turn dislodged some small plastic pots and a wooden cup full of make-up brushes. In a matter of seconds half the contents of Debbie's personal toilette had rolled off the dressing table and bounced across the bedroom floor. The cacophony had the desired effect. Debbie threw the pillow across the bed and sat bolt upright, her hair sticking to one side of her face.

'Molly, what on earth are you playing at?' she shouted angrily. I jumped onto the bed and stood across her legs, meowing in the most commanding tone I could manage. Debbie leant over and switched on her bedside lamp, looking at me irritably. 'Molly, what is it?' I jumped down from the bed and scratched at her bedroom door, looking at her over my shoulder. She sighed and swung her legs over the side of the bed. 'This had better be good, Molls.'

I ran down the stairs to the landing. Debbie followed at an infuriatingly slow pace, pulling on her dressing gown as she stumbled sleepily along the hall. I ran to the end of the hallway and waited for her at the top of the stairs to the café. As she got nearer, Debbie noticed the piece of plyboard lying on the floor.

'Molly, where do you think you're going? You're not allowed down there,' she said sternly. I walked over the plyboard and placed one foot on the first step, trying to entice her to come after me. 'Hey, Molly, I said you're not allowed down there.' She moved along the dark hallway and bent down to scoop me up. As she was about to lift me off the floor, she stopped. She stood up straight and sniffed. 'Oh, my God, is that gas?' she said, suddenly alert.

She raced past me down the stairs past me and I heard her run into the kitchen below.

'Oh, my God, the gas is leaking! What do I do?' she shrieked.

As I ran after her into the kitchen I saw that the pool of water underneath the boiler had spread across the kitchen floor. The air was thick with the pungent smell of gas, making my throat constrict and my eyes water. Debbie was standing in front of the boiler, one hand over her mouth in shock.

'Windows!' she shouted, and ran to the back of the kitchen to throw open the windows onto the alley. Then she grabbed the key to the back door and opened that too. She ran past me into the café and did the same in there, and soon the cool night breeze was blowing from the cobbled street in front to the alley at the back. Debbie stood by the kitchen door, swinging it back and forth by the handle, to increase the flow of fresh air into the room. The smell of gas quickly began to disperse, although the ominous hissing sound and the dripping of water onto the kitchen floor continued.

'Sophie!' she exclaimed suddenly. She closed the kitchen door and stood for a moment with her hand on the key, looking uncertain. 'Door open or door shut,

Molly?' she asked me desperately. I chirruped helplessly, wishing I knew which was the correct answer.
'You're right, Molly. Better to leave it open. You'll
watch out for burglars, won't you? I'll just be a second.'
I stood dutifully by the open door while Debbie
sprinted through the kitchen, then took the stairs two
at a time up to the flat. I could hear her shouting as she
ran along the hallway, 'Sophie! You need to wake up,
sweetheart. We've got a gas leak!'

A few moments later Debbie came tearing down
the stairs again, a dishevelled Sophie staggering sleepily behind her. Sophie screwed up her face as the smell
of gas hit her for the first time.

'Right, everybody onto the street,' Debbie ordered.

'Are you kidding, Mum? It's freezing out there.
Can't we just wait inside?' Sophie protested.

'Sophie. In case you hadn't noticed, we have a gas
leak, which could not only be poisonous, but is also
highly flammable. No, we cannot wait inside.' Debbie
bustled Sophie through the café door and out into the
cobbles. 'Come on, Molly, you need to come with us,'
she said impatiently, as I stood in the middle of the
café twitching my tail. 'Molly! Come on!' Debbie
shouted, her patience wearing thin. She dashed back
inside and tried to put her arms around me to lift me
up, but I wriggled and twisted out of her grip. As soon
as I had struggled free I ran back towards the stairs.

'Molly, what are you playing at? You need to come outside!' Debbie had never shouted at me like this before, but I was not about to let her anger deter me.

'She wants to get her kittens, Mum,' I heard Sophie say from the street. 'She doesn't want to leave them upstairs.'

Debbie groaned. 'Oh, of course, the kittens.' I could hear the exasperation in her voice.

I started to creep stealthily up the stairs, knowing that, if necessary, I could carry all the kittens to safety without her help.

'Okay, Molly – fair enough, but we'll have to be quick. Sophie, you stay there and don't move.'

'Are you kidding, Mum? I'm not going to stand out here on my own in the middle of the night! Besides, there are five kittens, and only one of you. It'll be quicker if I come.' Sophie was standing in the café doorway, hands on her hips, silhouetted by the street light behind. Debbie stood between us, clutching her hair as she tried to decide what to do. Still waiting on the stairs, I was losing patience with her procrastinating.

'Oh, all right then, come on!' Debbie cried, and the three of us stampeded upstairs to the flat. 'I'll need to find the carrier,' Debbie gasped, trying to catch her breath after running up the stairs for the second time in a matter of minutes. 'And then I'll need to join the gym,' she panted, as she steadied herself against the banister.

Sophie and I left her throwing coats and shoes out of the hallway cupboard as we ran into the living room. All the kittens were inside the cardboard box, fast asleep and blissfully unaware of the drama unfolding around them.

'Got it!' Debbie shouted in a voice that was verging on hysterical. She appeared in the living-room door-way, triumphantly clutching the carrier, even more flustered and red-faced than she had been before. She ran across the room to the cardboard box, unlocking the front of the carrier as she went. 'Right, come on Soph, gently does it,' she said.

The kittens started to squirm as she and Sophie picked them up, one by one, and placed them swiftly inside the carrier. By the time all five were inside they were wide awake, mewing and clambering over each other, confused at finding themselves incarcerated in a plastic box. I stayed close to the carrier as Debbie used both hands to lift it and we made our way, in a clumsy huddle, back along the hallway and down the narrow staircase.

Outside on the street, Debbie plonked the carrier down on the cobbles and sighed with relief. 'They're heavier than they look, you know!' she said to Sophie, by way of explanation for her shortness of breath. She slipped her hand into her dressing-gown pocket and pulled out her phone.

It was chilly outside and I could see goosebumps on Debbie's legs as she stood next to a shivering Sophie. She pressed the screen of her phone, then held it to her ear.

'Come on, come on – please pick up,' she whispered, bouncing up and down on the spot in agitation. She stopped moving suddenly and I heard a faint voice at the other end of the line. 'Oh, hi, John. I'm really sorry to call you so late. It's Debbie.'

29

We huddled in the café doorway, under the eerie orange light of a street lamp. Sophie rested her head on Debbie's shoulder, shivering in her thin cotton pyjamas. Every now and then a breeze wafted the smell of gas over to us, making my eyes prickle. As we waited, the kittens grew agitated, stumbling over each other as they tried to get to the front of the cat carrier. It felt strange to be on the street again, after so many weeks confined to the flat. My ears swivelled in alarm at sounds that had once been the familiar backdrop to my life: owls screeching in the churchyard, and cats yowling as they squared up for a fight in some distant passageway.

After about ten minutes we heard a car engine in a nearby street. Soon a pair of headlights appeared at the end of the parade, approaching slowly along the cobbles.

'This must be him!' Debbie whispered, lifting Sophie's head off her shoulder and stepping out of the doorway. She waved, squinting in the headlights' beams. 'Hi.' She smiled apologetically as John climbed out of the van. 'I can't thank you enough for coming out. I didn't know what else to do.'

John's eyes were puffy with sleep and, although his lips wore a thin smile, he did not return her greeting. He heaved his tool bag from the passenger seat onto his shoulder. 'Quite the street party you're having here,' he said, glancing at Sophie, at me and at the carrier full of kittens.

'Well, yes, because of the gas,' Debbie explained nervously. 'I got Sophie up, but then Molly wanted to go back for the kittens, so we had to get them too. But then I couldn't find the carrier, and I was out of breath from the stairs and I really need to do more exercise . . .'

John stared past Debbie blankly, ignoring her words as he walked towards the doorway. 'Very sensible, Molly,' he said, when Debbie finally paused for breath. 'You mustn't leave the kittens inside if there's a gas leak.' He bent down to stroke me and I purred, aware of Debbie looking crestfallen as she stood behind him.

'Well, obviously I would have gone back for the kittens anyway. I mean, I wouldn't have left them in there,' she stammered.

John straightened up, looking into the café. 'Shall I take a look then?' he said, cutting her off mid-sentence.

'Oh, of course – I mean, yes, please; thank you,' she babbled gratefully. John switched his torch on and walked inside. 'Shall I put the lights on for you?' she called as we followed him into the café.

'Not yet,' he replied brusquely. 'Don't want the place to go up in flames, do you?'

'Oh, no, of course – I knew that.' She sounded girlishly eager to please.

Sophie headed for a table in the corner of the café and placed the carrier of fidgeting kittens on the floor. Debbie trailed John into the kitchen, continuing to talk to his back.

'I'll never forget that advert on TV when I was younger: "If you can smell gas" and all that – scared the life out of me. "Don't use switches," it said, and that's always stayed with me. Never forgotten it.'

From the shadow of the serving counter I watched as John began to take the boiler apart, resolutely ignoring Debbie. I wished there was something I could do to stop her talking; it was obvious that he was finding her anxious prattle irritating.

After a few minutes the hissing noise stopped. 'The gas is off,' John said. 'I suggest we keep the windows open for a while, but it's safe to go upstairs, if you want to go back to bed.'

Debbie breathed a sigh of relief. 'Did you hear that, Soph? You can go back to bed now,' she called through the doorway.

Sophie was hunched on a chair with her head propped against the wall, hugging her knees to her chest. She did not acknowledge Debbie's words, but I heard her chair scrape on the flagstones as she stood up.

'Oh, take the kittens up too, would you, Soph?' Debbie pleaded. Sophie grunted a half-hearted objection, before picking up the carrier and stumbling towards the stairs. I heard the kittens mewing in protest as it bumped against every step on the way up to the flat. 'Night-night, love, I'll be up soon,' Debbie called from the foot of the stairs, her voice sounding artificially upbeat. There was no response from Sophie, and Debbie sighed.

'You know, you really shouldn't have left it this long. I did warn you that the boiler needed replacing as a matter of urgency,' John said coldly, once Debbie had returned to the kitchen.

Debbie hung her head in shame. 'I know, I know. I was planning to do it. It's just, what with the refurbishment and everything else, I hadn't got round to it yet . . .' she trailed off. John had turned his back to her again, wordlessly dismissing her excuses. Debbie sat down on a stool, looking despondent.

'On the bright side, you're very lucky you caught this when you did. Could have been a lot worse, if the gas had been running all night.'

Debbie shuddered. 'I can't even bear to think about it. Thank goodness for Molly.' At this, John glanced quizzically over his shoulder. 'She came into my room and woke me up,' she elaborated, visibly relieved that John had, at last, shown an interest in something she had said. 'She wouldn't take no for an answer. Patting my face, knocking things off my dressing table – it was like an episode of *Lassie* up there!'

John raised his eyebrows and smiled for the first time since he had arrived. 'Well, good for Molly. You've got a lot to thank her for.'

Debbie shivered as a gust of wind from the alley blew through the kitchen, rattling the window blinds. Rubbing her arms against the chill, she contemplated the puddle of rusty water on the floor. 'I suppose I might as well make myself useful,' she sighed, taking a mop and bucket from the cupboard.

I crept around the side of the serving counter to watch them through the doorway. John was taking the boiler apart, piece by piece, painstakingly removing rusty metal panels and segments of pipe. Debbie made her way slowly across the floor, swinging the mop back and forth, squeezing it out into a bucket. She looked almost comically dishevelled in her faded dressing gown and damp slippers. One of her cheeks was pillow-creased, and a clump of hair stood up at the back of her head. I saw her cast a furtive glance at her reflection in the kitchen window and surreptitiously try to smooth her hair with the palm of her hand.

The awkwardness between them was palpable. John had resumed his tight-lipped frostiness. And, having been unable to stop talking when he first arrived, it seemed as if Debbie had run out of things to say. Crouching between the counter and the doorway, I racked my brain for a way to defuse the tension between them.

'That's the gas and water disconnected,' John said at last, wiping his forehead with the back of his hand. 'I'll do my best to source a replacement for you tomorrow. Until then, I'm afraid everything's going to have to stay as it is.' He addressed his words to the boiler rather than to Debbie, while she nodded gratefully, fiddling with the mop handle.

'Well, thank you so much,' she said after a moment's silence, when it had become clear that John had nothing further to say on the matter.

The first streaks of orange and pink were appearing in the sky outside, and an outburst of chatter from some nearby magpies pierced the air. John had started to pack up his tools. Whatever Debbie might think of me, I knew that if I was going to act, it would have to be now or never. I sidled over to John and wound myself around his leg.

'Oh, hello, Molly,' he said, giving me a cursory stroke. I saw Debbie glance sideways, surprised to see that I had not followed Sophie and the kittens upstairs. I loitered by John's feet and, as soon as he turned away to pick something up, I jumped into his tool bag. 'Come on, girl, out you get,' he coaxed, lifting me gently under my tummy and placing me on the floor. I immediately jumped back in and looked at him mischievously. 'Molly, come on now.'

He was starting to get annoyed, and I was conscious of Debbie glaring at me, her surprise turning to embarrassment. John lifted me out for a second time and zipped his bag shut. He hoisted the bag onto his shoulder and began to walk towards the café door. My tail twitched; I sensed that, if Debbie let him leave without the two of them clearing the air, the damage would be irreparable. I trotted after him and darted between his feet as he walked, causing him to stumble and trip.

'Oh, Molly, be careful!' he exclaimed, exasperated. I dashed in front of him and meowed plaintively. He looked down at me and his irritation was plain to see; he looked exhausted and annoyed. I began to despair

– things were not going to plan, and it looked as if my actions had succeeded only in making John crosser than before. He opened his mouth to speak and I closed my eyes, prepared for the inevitable telling-off. But instead of John's voice, I heard Debbie's.

She was giggling. I opened my eyes and peered around John's leg, to see Debbie leaning against the kitchen doorway with her arms folded. 'I think Molly's telling you to stay for a cup of tea,' she laughed.

John put his bag down on the floor. 'I thought you'd never ask,' he smiled.

Debbie put the kettle on, while John moved around the café closing the doors and windows. The pink dawn was spreading upwards through the sky and the first rays of sunlight had broken over the roofs opposite.

'I love the new look of the place, by the way,' John said, as the café's bright interior emerged from the gloom. 'Especially those paw prints on the floor. Nice touch!'

'You can probably guess who was responsible for those,' Debbie answered drily from the kitchen. 'Molly's our design director, as well as our fire safety officer.' She carried two mugs of tea through the café and placed them on the table in the bay window.

Much as I wanted to stay and eavesdrop on their conversation, I had a feeling that my presence would be a distraction. They had talked enough about me for one night, and there were other things they needed to discuss. I tiptoed unnoticed past their table and crept upstairs, leaving them sipping tea in the golden dawn light.

30

I squeezed into the cardboard box, trying not to wake the sleeping kittens. As I lay down alongside Eddie, he instinctively twisted towards me, nestling his face into my neck. I licked the top of his head and he began to purr drowsily, stretching out his legs between mine.

Looking down at his outstretched body, it was impossible to ignore the similarities between Eddie and his father, the tomcat. The resemblance was uncanny: a square face framed by white whiskers, a bib of white on his chest, and legs that, for now at least, appeared too long for his body. But, as he grew, I realized that it wasn't just the tomcat's physical features that Eddie had inherited. His temperament was also unmistakeably like his father's. There was a selflessness about him, a willingness to put the needs of others before his own, which made my heart swell with pride. I sometimes watched him at feeding time, waiting patiently while his sisters ate, never doubting that there would be enough food to go round. It made my heart catch in my throat to witness his generosity of spirit, and the way it mirrored the chivalry his father had shown me in the alley.

My remorse for the way I had treated the tomcat had never left me. Since the birth of the kittens I had had less time to dwell on it, but the moments when I glimpsed their father's traits in them still brought me up short. I sometimes wondered how they would react if they were ever to meet him. Would they instinctively know he was their father, or would they think him a stranger – perhaps even consider him a threat? The pleasure and pride I took in watching my kittens grow would forever be tinged with sadness at what I, and they, had lost. In my desperation to find an owner to replace Margery I had, unwittingly, sacrificed my opportunity for feline companionship. I could not wish for a better owner than Debbie, but I would always wonder whether, if I had done things differently, the tomcat might still be living in the alley and might still be a part of my life.

It was, in part, this regret that had motivated me to bring Debbie and John together that night. It was too late for me and the tomcat, but I wanted Debbie to make an informed choice: to know what she was giving up, if she ruled out the possibility of a relationship with

John. As I started to drift out of consciousness, my mind wandered back to my conversation with Nancy, as I had prepared for my journey to Stourton. 'Humans always think they know what they want, but they don't always know what they *need*. You can be the one to show them,' she had told me, as we sat in the play-ground on the edge of Rob's estate. At the time I had not understood what she meant, so preoccupied was I with the daunting challenge that lay ahead of me. But as I was lulled to sleep by the sound of Eddie's heart-beat thumping against my chest, I wondered whether I had done just that for Debbie: I had shown her that what she needed was John.

'Debbie, are you up there? What's going on? Why aren't you open?'

Jo was in the café stairwell, shouting up to the flat. The kittens began to stir around me, emerging unwill-ingly from the fog of sleep. I heard Debbie stumble out of her bedroom in response to Jo's shouts, having over-slept after the previous night's drama. Trying not to disturb the kittens, I climbed out of the box and walked to the hallway, just as Jo's worried face appeared above the plyboard at the top of the stairs.

'I've been calling you, but it kept going to voicemail, so I let myself in with the spare key. Why aren't you open – is everything all right?'

Debbie staggered down the stairs from her bed-room. 'We can't open today. We've got no gas or hot water,' she explained, lifting the upended ironing board out of her way. The contents of the cupboard were still strewn across the hallway floor, after Debbie's frantic efforts to locate the cat carrier during the night.

'Boiler finally packed in?' Jo asked. Debbie nodded sheepishly. Jo's eyes flashed. 'Oh, Debs, you knew that needed to be sorted out!'

'I know, Jo. Please, I had enough of a telling-off from John about it last night.'

'John's been round? Last night?' Jo's mouth curled into a smile; I sensed that, like me, she also nursed hopes on this subject. 'So, it's not all bad news then. I'll put the kettle on, then you can tell me all about it.' She bustled past Debbie into the kitchen.

I followed Debbie into the living room, where she slumped, yawning, onto a dining chair. The sound of voices had finally roused the kittens and they trotted towards the kitchen in hope of breakfast. I could hear their excited mewing as they tried to get Jo's attention.

'Oh, all right kitties, here you go,' she said, filling their bowls with cat biscuits. A couple of minutes later, Jo put a cup of coffee and a slice of toast on the table in front of Debbie.

'Thanks, Jo,' Debbie murmured, taking a bite.

'So go on then, tell me what happened.' Jo's eyes

glinted with eager anticipation. Debbie rubbed her face. 'Well, around three a.m. Molly came and told me the gas was leaking.'

Jo did a double-take. 'Molly told you the gas was leaking?' she repeated.

Debbie took a sip of coffee. 'Well, she didn't *tell* me, obviously, but she must have known something was wrong, because she kept waking me up, wanting me to follow her downstairs.'

Jo cast an admiring look in my direction, then listened avidly while Debbie recounted the night's events. She sat in open-mouthed horror when Debbie described the dripping boiler and hissing gas pipe; chuckled as she explained how we had all stood on the street, waiting for John to arrive; and couldn't contain her glee when Debbie admitted that she and John had stayed up past dawn drinking tea. Having finished her story, Debbie stifled another yawn.

'So, what's next?' Jo asked.

'I've got to speak to the bank today about increasing the loan. John said he's going to try and find us a replacement this week—'

'I'm not talking about the boiler!' Jo cut in, exasperated. 'I mean what's next with John?'

Debbie looked at the table bashfully. 'I don't know, Jo – probably nothing. We didn't exactly discuss our future plans. It was hardly the time or place.'

'Are you kidding, Debs? He came out to help you in the middle of the night. He's seen you in your dressing gown! That's practically married, in my book.'

Debbie winced. 'Please, don't remind me.' She took a bite of toast, avoiding Jo's piercing gaze. 'I suppose I do owe him, after what he did for us,' she said at last, to emphatic nodding from Jo. 'Maybe I should offer to take him for a drink, to say thanks.'

Jo was silent, but I saw her smile as she took a sip from her mug.

John returned to the café a few days later to fit the new boiler. The walls in the flat shook with banging and drilling from the kitchen below, followed eventually by gurgling in the pipes as the heating system refilled.

It was late afternoon by the time Debbie came upstairs to the flat, and she disappeared immediately into the bathroom to run herself a bath. I was desperate to know how she and John had got on with each other, but I had to wait until she and Sophie ate dinner before my curiosity was satisfied.

Debbie looked refreshed in clean pyjamas, her hair still damp from the bath, as she placed two bowls of pasta on the dining table.

'Soph, just out of interest, how would you feel if, one evening, I went out for a drink?' Her voice was studiedly casual, but my ears pricked up.

'With Jo?' Sophie asked disinterestedly, scrolling across the screen of her phone.

Debbie paused. 'No, not with Jo. With John.' Her eyes flicked nervously across the table.

'John? Who's John?' A distracted frown was forming between Sophie's brows.

'John the plumber. Who replaced the boiler.'

Sophie looked up, her face a study in befuddlement. 'John the plumber?' Debbie nodded. Sophie looked perplexed for a moment, then shrugged. 'Yeah, whatever.'

'Whatever?' Debbie repeated. 'Is that "whatever" as in "I don't mind", or "whatever" as in "I do mind"?'

Sophie looked infuriated and amused in equal measure. 'It means "whatever", Mum, as in "Do whatever you like". You can go for a drink with whoever you want to go for a drink with.'

Debbie seemed troubled, unsure whether Sophie's encouragement was genuine or sarcastic. Sophie lifted a forkful of pasta into her mouth with one hand while tapping her phone with the other, oblivious to her mother's discomfort.

'But, you wouldn't find it . . . strange at all?' Debbie persisted.

Sophie put her fork down on her plate and looked calmly at Debbie. 'Mum, like I said, I don't mind. If you want to go for a drink with John, then go for a drink with John. It's about time you got yourself out there.' Debbie smiled, visibly touched by Sophie's response. 'Otherwise you're going to turn into one of those crazy women who live alone and talk to their cats. Let's be honest, you're not far off it already.'

Debbie's smile faded. She opened her mouth to protest, but hesitated, looking down at her food in silence. From my position on the arm of the sofa I delivered my haughtiest stare at Sophie, bristling at the suggestion that there was anything crazy about the way in which Debbie talked to me.

'Okay, I just wanted to check. Thanks, Soph,' Debbie said meekly, and Sophie shrugged again.

John's name was not mentioned again, and as the week went on I began to despair of Debbie following through on her plan to take him for a drink. A few nights later, however, she disappeared up to her bedroom after work. I could hear drawers being opened and closed, and her cries of frustration made me think that her evening's plans must involve something other than a takeaway with Jo. My curiosity piqued, I trotted upstairs and peered round her bedroom door, to see Debbie standing next to the bed in her dressing gown, pink-cheeked and agitated. She had emptied the contents of her wardrobe onto the bed, where the clothes lay in a tangled heap on the quilt. Sophie was sitting at the dressing table, her chin resting on her hand, looking bored.

'How I can have so many clothes, and yet still have nothing to wear?' Debbie whined.

I jumped onto the bed, treading carefully around the mounds of sweaters, skirts and trousers.

'You've got loads of stuff to wear, Mum, you've just got to make a decision,' Sophie replied glumly.

Debbie dropped hopelessly onto the edge of the bed. She looked close to tears, so I scaled a mound of knitwear to rub against her arm. She stroked me despondently while Sophie, tutting with frustration at her mother's indecisiveness, leant over to tackle the mountain of clothes.

'No; no; possibly; no,' Sophie said, assessing each item in turn before placing it back on the bed. 'This is quite nice.' She held up a pink V-necked top.

Debbie took it and held it in front of her body. 'You don't think it's a bit . . . revealing?' she asked, an uncertain smile playing around her lips.

'Well, if you're worried, why don't you wear this under it?' Sophie replied calmly, plucking a cream-coloured camisole from the pile and handing it to Debbie. 'Or something on top . . . No, Mum, not that!' – Debbie had picked up a chunky-knit cardigan – 'a scarf or something. You could wear your nice jeans, the fitted ones.'

Debbie was unconvinced, but Sophie's enthusiasm gave her the confidence to try the ensemble. While she changed, I climbed onto a pile of rejected clothes, circling a few times to form a nest. I lay down and began to wash.

'What do you think?' Debbie asked, standing in front of her full-length mirror. It was not often that I saw her wear anything other than her work uniform of black trousers and nondescript sweater. The deep pink of her top brought out the blue of her eyes. 'Are you sure it's not too much, Soph?' She smiled, girlishly self-conscious, and for a moment I glimpsed Sophie in her face.

Sophie eyed her mother up and down dispassionately. 'No, Mum, you actually look all right.'

Debbie sighed and stared at her reflection, the look on her face suggesting resignation rather than satisfaction.

'Hurry up, Mum – you don't want to keep John waiting,' Sophie teased. My ears pricked up. I was delighted, at last, to hear confirmation that Debbie's plans involved John.

Debbie glanced at her watch and gasped. 'I've just remembered why I never wear heels!' she muttered as she sat on the end of the bed, struggling to force her feet into a pair of shoes. She slipped on her jacket and grabbed her handbag. 'Don't stay up too late,' she instructed Sophie, who rolled her eyes, but said nothing.

In the hallway, Debbie blew us both a kiss before disappearing downstairs and letting herself out through the café. I sat at the top of the stairs, listening as the clicking of her heels on the cobbles faded into the distance.

Much later that evening, after Sophie had gone to bed, I was woken by the sound of the café door slamming. Debbie climbed the stairs and groaned with relief as she slipped her shoes off. I stepped into the hall to greet her.

'Good evening, Molly,' she smiled and I trotted towards her, my tail raised in salutation.

The giggly tone of Debbie's voice suggested the evening had gone well, and I hoped she would want to talk about it. She poured herself a glass of water at the kitchen sink before hobbling to the sofa, where I jumped onto the cushion next to her.

'What is it, Molly? Why are you looking at me like that?' she asked. I purred encouragingly. 'Well, you can purr all you like. I'm not a crazy woman who talks to cats, you know. At least, not yet.' She chuckled. 'And, besides, a lady will never kiss and tell.' She pressed my nose gently but firmly with the tip of her finger, before drinking her water in one long gulp. When the glass was empty she pushed herself upright. 'Time I got to bed,' she announced, wincing at the pain in her feet.

My tail twitched with frustration as I watched her limp out of the room. I desperately wanted to hear details about how the evening had gone, and her refusal to talk left me feeling thwarted. She made her way slowly upstairs to the bedroom, and I smiled inwardly when I heard her groan, upon finding her bed still covered in piles of clothes.

31

The week after Debbie and John's date began like any other. Sophie rushed out on Monday morning, late for her bus; Debbie ate a piece of toast at the kitchen sink, before disappearing downstairs to work; and I spent the day in the flat, supervising the kittens. They were almost three months old now, and although I had done what I could to curb their more boisterous tendencies, I couldn't help but notice the damage they had wrought around the living room: the frayed fabric on the sofa corners, the chewed rug tassels and the scratched wallpaper.

Debbie had never said a word to admonish them for their behaviour, but my heart always sank when I uncovered new evidence of their destructiveness; it meant the time was surely coming when Debbie would rehome them. I knew the kittens would thrive in their own homes, with loving owners and the space they needed to develop into mature, independent cats. I knew it would be wrong to keep them cooped up together with me in the tiny flat. And yet, in spite of all that, my heart ached whenever I thought of being separated from them.

When Debbie returned to the flat that evening she looked tired and worn out. She flopped onto the sofa next to Sophie, kicking off her shoes.

'Good day at school?' Debbie asked.

Sophie shrugged. 'It was all right. Just teachers stressing about exams, as usual.'

Debbie patted Sophie's arm encouragingly. 'Nearly there now, Soph, just a few more weeks to get through, then you can relax.' She flicked through the pile of post that she had carried upstairs with her, sighing when she saw the postmark on one of the envelopes. 'Another letter from Stourton District Council. I wonder what demand they've come up with this time.' The previous few weeks had been punctuated by the arrival of letters from the town council, each one raising a new objection to Debbie's plans for the cat café. She grimaced as she ripped open the envelope.

'Oh, my goodness!' she said, scanning the letter's contents.

'What?' Sophie replied. Debbie's mouth had fallen open and her lips were pale. 'Mum, what's wrong? You're worrying me.'

'I can't believe it. Nothing's wrong, Soph. Read this, will you?' She handed the letter to Sophie, sliding forward to perch on the edge of the sofa.

Not wanting to be left out of whatever crisis was brewing, I jumped off the windowsill and went to sit by Debbie's feet.

Sophie's eyes flicked across the letter, her brow knitted in concentration. But, as she handed the letter back to Debbie, she grinned. 'They're giving you permission to open the cat café. They've said yes, Mum!'

Debbie leapt up, her sudden movement sending me and the kittens scattering across the room in panic. She was clutching the letter close to her chest, as if frightened that someone might snatch it from her. She paced back and forth across the rug, rereading phrases from the letter aloud, reassuring herself that she hadn't misunderstood their meaning.

'"As long as all the cats in question are the owner's pets and will not to be offered to the public for adoption, it will not be necessary to obtain a licence for the cat café from Animal Welfare."' Debbie emitted a gasp of disbelief. 'I can't believe it! After everything they put us through, it turns out all they needed was confirmation that the cats belong to me and won't be rehomed!'

She let out a high-pitched squeal and began to jump up and down on the rug as the letter's meaning sank in. The kittens, responding to her excitement, began to chase each other in frenzied circuits around the living room, but Debbie didn't seem to notice them. '"Molly's Cat Café". It'll be your café, Molls – yours and the kittens'. What will the old battleaxe make of that, eh?' Debbie smiled at me, her eyes glinting. Behind her, Purdy, hotly pursued by Abby, shot up the living-room curtain, startling Debbie and making her shriek.

Sophie stood up and touched her mother's arm lightly. 'Maybe you should sit down while you let it sink in, Mum,' she said soothingly.

'Sit down? How can I sit down! This calls for a celebration,' Debbie shouted gleefully, waving the letter in the air. She ran into the kitchen, where I could hear her rummaging noisily through the kitchen cupboards. 'Why is there never any champagne when you need it?' she shouted.

'Because you drank it the night the kittens were born,' Sophie replied drily.

'Well, I should have bought some more to replace it,' Debbie yelled. 'Anyone would think we don't have enough things to celebrate in this flat!' A few moments later she reappeared, carrying a bottle and two wine glasses on a tray. 'Right, I'm afraid this is the best I can do,' she said, placing the tray on the dining table.

'Oh, Mum, what is that?' Sophie asked, picking up the bottle dubiously. 'Lambrini Cherry? Are you kidding?'

'I know, but it's the best we've got. I won it at the tombola at the school Christmas fair, remember?' She peeled off a paper raffle ticket, which had been taped to the neck of the bottle, then poured the fizzing pink liquid into the glasses.

'To Molly's Cat Café!' Debbie toasted merrily, clinking her glass against Sophie's.

Sophie took a sip, winced, then ran into the kitchen to spit her mouthful into the sink. 'Urgh, that's rank, Mum,' she shouted, rinsing her mouth with tap water.

Debbie picked up the bottle and examined the label. 'Hmm. Expiry date was October of last year. That might explain the vinegary tang. Never mind.' She took the bottle into the kitchen and emptied it down the plughole.

The following fortnight passed in a state of frenetic activity as Debbie prepared for a final inspection by Environmental Health. She spent her days making adjustments to the café, while I listened to the goings-on from behind the plyboard panel at the top of the stairs. The installation of a new gate next to the serving counter – designed to block feline access to the kitchen – was of little interest to me, but my ears pricked up with curiosity when I heard her accept a large delivery from a pet-supplies van parked outside. When John was set to work in the alleyway with a saw and long pieces of timber, I pressed my nose against the living-room window, eager to see what he was building, but all I could make out were the offcuts of wood that he threw into the recycling bin. Debbie spent her evenings in the flat with Sophie, whose exams were at last finished, and together they devised dishes for the new cat-themed menu.

'How about Tummy Tickler Teacakes?' she asked Sophie, tapping her cheek thoughtfully with her pen.

Sophie nodded enthusiastically. 'Frosty Paws Cake-Pops?' she suggested in return, while Debbie scribbled keenly on her notepad.

'We've got to have some tuna on there somewhere. It's Molly's favourite, after all,' Debbie insisted. 'What about tuna-melt muffins, with grated cheese?' Sophie suggested. 'Perfect,' Debbie smiled, as my mouth began to water.

When the day of the inspection arrived, Debbie was agitated. She paced around the flat, unable to eat any breakfast, and smiled wanly when Sophie shouted, 'Don't worry, Mum, it'll be fine,' on her way out.

At the appointed time, Debbie ran down to the café and I listened from the top of the stairs as she showed the Environmental Health Inspector around the premises. She sounded calm and businesslike as she answered his questions, proudly displaying her colour-coded cleaning materials – red for the cat area, blue for the kitchen – and showing him our vaccination certificates. At last Debbie walked the inspector to the café door, bidding him farewell and closing it carefully behind him. Then I heard her squeal and she raced up the stairs.

'Guess what, Molly – we passed!' she shrieked, leaping over the plyboard panel and scooping me up into the air.

Her excitement was infectious and I let her spin me around in the air, even though it made me dizzy.

'Would you like to go downstairs and explore your café?' Debbie asked the kittens as they frolicked around her, sensing her mood. With mock-solemnity, she removed the plyboard barrier and ushered them onto the top step.

Purdy led the charge, with the others following behind, all of them torn between excitement and fear. I brought up the rear of the procession alongside Maisie, who preferred to stick close to me for reassurance. When she reached the bottom step, Purdy paused, suddenly cowed by the size and unfamiliarity of the café. Behind her, the kittens formed a nervous queue. I slipped past them to stand on the café floor, encouraging them to follow me. They inched slowly forwards, taking cautious, precise steps across the flagstones as they gazed around them, their eyes wide with wonder.

Only when they had all stepped onto the flagstones did I turn to look too. The café felt instantly familiar. I quickly spotted my trail of paw prints on the floor, and my gingham cushion in the window. But dotted around the café, between the tables and chairs, were scratching posts, polythene play tunnels and platform towers. Debbie had placed two cosy armchairs in front of the stove, each with a cushion reading 'Reserved for the cat' propped against its back. On the floor between the armchairs was a basket full of cat toys, which Abby and Bella wasted no time in emptying onto the floor, where they began to bat a catnip mouse between them.

When I turned around I saw that John had fixed wooden planks to one of the walls in a zigzag formation, to make a walkway that led up to a small hammock suspended from the ceiling. Purdy immediately mounted the lowest plank and, flicking her tail from side to side, sashayed up to the hammock at the top. She climbed inside and stared triumphantly down at her siblings.

Debbie and I stood in the middle of the café, watching them play. 'Do you think they like it, Molly?' she asked, and I purred at her. I knew they loved it. I did too.

32

Molly's Cat Café opened for business the following week. I took my role as the café's figurehead seriously, sitting on my cushion in the window, looking out onto the street with pride. There was a noticeable buzz around the café on launch day: Debbie had draped bunting in the window, and a large chalkboard stood on the pavement outside, declaring the café 'Open for Coffee, Cake and Cuddles'. Inquisitive passers-by gathered in front of the glass to peer inside, and a glimpse of the kittens was often enough to tempt them through the door.

Just before lunchtime, my meditative daze was interrupted by the sound of wheels rattling on the cobblestones outside. I opened my eyes to see the old lady with the shopping trolley striding past the café, her eyes narrowed and her lips pursed. I instinctively braced myself for confrontation, but she kept her eyes fixed on the pavement, determined not to look in my direction. Watching her trundle away, I felt a glow of satisfaction. Behind me, Debbie was happily handing out menus and taking orders, while delighted customers played with the kittens. The old woman's attempt to sabotage the café had failed, and there was nothing more she could do to hurt us.

In those early days I sometimes had to open my eyes and look around, to be sure that the cat café was not a dream. Ever since my incarceration in the flat I had prepared myself for the worst, imagining the regretful look on Debbie's face as she broke the news that she had found new homes for the kittens and me. I had rehearsed the scene in my mind so many times that it felt real, and I would sometimes wake from a nap with a jolt, convinced that when I opened my eyes I would find that the kittens had gone.

About a week after the café's relaunch, I was woken by the tinkling of the bell on the door. Still half-asleep and momentarily panicked, I scanned the café to check that all the kittens were present. Reassured that there was no cause for alarm, I watched drowsily as a woman pushed an elderly lady in a wheelchair through the café to a table.

I lowered my chin to my paws and closed my eyes, but something prevented me from drifting off. There was a scent in the air that I recognized, but could not place. Unable to sleep, I jumped down from the armchair and followed the scent trail across the café. Unaware that I was stalking up behind them, the two customers murmured to each other as they perused their menus. My feeling of unease was growing, evoking a sensation that I could only describe as homesickness. When I was a few paces away from the customers, I stopped dead in my tracks. My mind and senses were suddenly alert with recognition: the scent was lavender.

I padded around the side of the wheelchair to look at the figure inside it. An elderly woman was slumped low in the seat, her face hidden behind her menu. Feeling the hairs on the back of my neck start to stand up, I lifted a paw and tugged at the folds of skirt around the lady's ankles. She peered over the side of her chair, two rheumy blue eyes in a face framed by soft waves of silver.

'Well now, who's this?' she asked, extending one hand shakily towards me.

With my heart beating in my throat, I stepped forwards to sniff her papery skin. In that instant, a wave of emotion stronger than anything I had ever experienced surged through me and, before I even had time to think, I had leapt over the arm of the wheelchair and into the lady's lap.

'I think that cat likes you, Margery,' said the young woman at the table, as I rubbed my head ecstatically against the soft folds of Margery's cheek.

'I used to have a cat just like this,' she replied, clucking softly as she stroked my body. 'There, there, puss,' she whispered, and I purred so loudly that I thought my heart would burst.

When I pulled my back from Margery's face, I saw that Debbie had walked over to the table and was watching in amazement. 'This is Molly,' she said. 'I've only had her for a few months. She was a stray.'

'Oh, Molly, yes – that's her name!' Margery replied, her eyes still on me, her face breaking into a smile. 'Is that you, Molly?' She took hold of my face gently, between quivering hands. I purred and rubbed her fingers with my whiskers, wanting to leave her in no doubt of who I was.

So many times, since losing Margery, I had sought solace in memories of our life together. Imagining her smile, or the feel of her hands on my fur, had kept me going when I was alone and desperate. Remembering our happy times at home had given me faith that another loving owner might be out there, somewhere, if only I could find them. But, as time passed, Margery's image had faded, becoming pale and indistinct like the sun-bleached photographs she had kept on the mantelpiece. Then, when I could no longer call her image to mind, all that had remained was the memory of how she had made me feel: safe, and loved.

As Margery cradled me on her lap in the café, I felt transported back to my kittenhood, believing that nothing could hurt me while I was in her arms. My unhappy time at Rob's house, the lonely journey to Stourton, my bittersweet memories of life in the alley, even my joy at having the kittens – all fell away, and for a few blissful moments it was just me and Margery, and our love for each other. Just as it had been in the beginning.

I have no idea how long we remained like that, utterly absorbed in each other, feeling as if the world had shrunk to the chair that held us both.

Eventually, unwillingly, I started to become aware of the café around us. I heard hushed voices nearby, the sound of the kittens playing and somebody sniffing above my head. When at last I opened my eyes, I saw Debbie standing next to Margery's wheelchair, dabbing her cheek with a tissue.

'She moved into the care home last year. I knew she loved cats, so when I heard about this place I decided to bring her,' Margery's companion said quietly.

'Do you think Molly could really have been her cat?' Debbie whispered.

'She's got advanced dementia and gets confused by

a lot of things, but she seems pretty certain about this,' the carer replied.

'Molly does too,' Debbie agreed. 'I've never seen her react like this to a stranger before.'

Debbie brought Margery a pot of tea and a Cat's Whiskers cookie, pulling up a stool beside her wheelchair.

Margery took her hand. 'This is my cat Molly, you know,' she said, beaming at Debbie.

'I know, Margery. Isn't it lovely that you've found each other again?'

Margery's smile lit up her face.

'I wonder how she managed to find her way to Stourton,' Debbie prompted, at which Margery's brow furrowed. 'She's Molly, my cat,' she repeated.

I sensed her agitation, and knew that confusion was beginning to descend. I rubbed my head against her hand, trying to reassure her that we were together again, and that nothing else mattered.

All too soon it was time for Margery to leave. Debbie took a photograph of the two of us, before lifting me gently from Margery's lap. 'You will come back, I hope?' Debbie asked, as she walked them to the door.

The carer promised they would return soon. 'It's done her the world of good,' she smiled.

As Margery was wheeled past, she reached out and took Debbie's hand, grasping it tightly. 'She's my cat, you know,' she said, looking up into Debbie's face intently.

Debbie squeezed her hand and nodded. 'I know, Margery. Come back and see her soon.'

Over dinner that evening Debbie told Sophie about what had happened, her eyes filling with tears as she described our reunion. She passed her phone to Sophie, its screen displaying the photo of the two of us.

'Wow!' Sophie said, her eyes reddening. She was studying the photo closely when the phone beeped. 'It's a text from John, Mum,' Sophie said, handing the phone back to Debbie. 'He says you need to talk.'

33

Debbie unlocked the door and stood aside to let John in, gesturing towards the nearest table. Outside, the evening sky was heavy with low cloud, and a sharp wind whipped through the trees, heralding the arrival of a storm. In the dusky half-light of the café I crouched inside the cardboard box by the stove, trying to quell a feeling of foreboding in my stomach.

John smiled tensely at Debbie as he walked past her, but she remained resolutely aloof. Although I didn't understand what had caused this sudden coolness between them, I felt a twinge of guilt. I knew I had played a part in bringing them together, and I had done everything I could to encourage Debbie to trust John. If he had done something to betray her trust, would I have to bear some of the responsibility for that too?

He slung his jacket over a chair and sat down with his back to me. Debbie sat opposite him across a small table, her face pale but composed as she waited for him to speak.

'Thanks for letting me come at such short notice,' John began, sounding polite to the point of formality.

'So, what do we need to talk about?' Debbie replied briskly. She looked him in the eye, her gaze challenging him.

John sighed and pulled an envelope from the inside pocket of his jacket, sliding it across the table towards her. 'This came through my letterbox this morning,' he said quietly. 'I thought it was only fair to show you.'

Debbie took the single sheet of paper from the envelope. Her face remained impassive as she read, but I could see the page quiver with the trembling of her hands. When she had finished, she folded the letter up and slotted it back inside its envelope.

'Quite a read, isn't it?' she said coldly, placing the letter on the table between them. 'I notice that whoever wrote it was too much of a coward to sign it. But then, I suppose, poison-pen letters are always anonymous.' Her voice caught as she spoke and her eyes looked glassy.

I longed to comfort her, to jump into her lap and soothe her with my purr, but I knew this situation was beyond my power to fix. John's posture suggested that he was looking at her, waiting for her to continue.

'So I guess you're here to tell me that you don't want

anything more to do with me?' Debbie asked matter-of-factly. 'According to this' – she waved her hand dismissively at the letter – 'I'm planning to fleece you for your money, then do a runner. Because that's what I've done before, apparently.' She took a sharp intake of breath as if, by saying the words out loud, their meaning had hit her for the first time. Her eyes were defiant, but I could see what an effort it was taking for her to stay calm.

'I never said I believed it,' John replied quietly. 'I considered throwing it away and saying nothing about it. But I thought it was better to deal with . . . something like this . . . out in the open. I don't know who wrote it, but—'

'Oh, I know who wrote it,' Debbie cut in, her composure suddenly faltering. 'The same vicious old woman who tried to have us closed down by Environmental Health.' Her eyes had narrowed and her mouth twisted in a bitter smile. John remained motionless, looking at her across the table, and for a moment the room was silent but for the sound of the café awning flapping in the wind outside.

'Vicious old woman?' he repeated.

Debbie's eyes flashed at him. 'The wretched battle-axe who's always going up and down the parade, shooting me filthy looks, saying nasty things to Sophie in the street. The old bat has had it in for me since the moment we moved in. She even tried to run Molly down with her shopping trolley once.' She laughed mirthlessly, acknowledging the apparent absurdity of what she was saying. 'She said it was an accident and scurried away, but Sophie saw what happened, and it was deliberate. I knew the woman was crazy, but I didn't think she'd go this far.' The words poured out of her, betraying the resentment that she had kept pent up for so long. When she had finished speaking, her shoulders drooped and she looked down at her hands, avoiding John's gaze.

I wished I could see his face to gauge his reaction, but his back was squarely to me. He remained silent while he considered her words. 'An old woman with a shopping trolley?' he asked at last. Debbie nodded, still staring sadly at her hands. 'Red hair?'

She looked up. 'That's the one. Why, friend of yours, is she?' she asked sarcastically.

'Not exactly, but I'm pretty sure I know who you mean. She's lived in Stourton for as long as I can remember. Used to own this place in fact.'

Debbie fixed him with a stare. 'This place? You mean the café?'

John nodded. 'I used to come in here when I was a kid. She was always behind the counter.' Debbie stared at him, wide-eyed, impatient to hear more. 'She owned it with her husband, but then one day he disappeared, did a runner—' John stopped mid-sentence, realizing that he had unwittingly echoed the letter's accusation against Debbie. 'Anyway, according to town gossip, he'd run up huge debts: gambling, I think. The café was in their joint name, so when the bailiffs showed up, she had no choice but to sell. After that she seemed to take it upon herself to make other people's lives miserable. She was always making complaints, writing letters, reporting people to the police for no good reason. After a while no one took her seriously – everyone just ignored her.'

'Well, I can't ignore her, can I?' Debbie cut in sharply. 'The café nearly went under, thanks to her interference. I thought we were going to default on the mortgage. Sophie and I could have been homeless.' She swallowed a sob. 'And now she's played her trump card by scaring you off. I've got to hand it to her, she plays a good game.' She turned her head towards the window so that John could not see her tears.

'Who said anything about her scaring me off?' John replied quietly.

'Well, isn't that why you're here?' Debbie shot back defiantly. 'That's what "We need to talk" usually means. This is a small town. You couldn't risk getting involved with someone with my reputation.' She picked up the letter and waved it towards him. 'There's no smoke without fire, after all – isn't that what you think?'

I had never seen Debbie like this before, not even in the heat of an argument with Sophie. Her lips were white and, although she was crying, she looked like she was seething with rage. I held my breath, praying that John would see through her hostility and recognize the hurt that lay underneath. I willed him to say that he didn't believe what was written in the letter, that the old woman was crazy and that he trusted Debbie completely. But he didn't say anything. He was looking down at the table, seemingly in no rush to put her out of her misery.

'I know you don't get on with Sophie's dad,' he began slowly, 'but that's all I know. To be honest, it's never felt appropriate to ask. Your past is your private business—'

'Not any more, apparently,' Debbie interrupted, curtly.

John sighed and I saw his shoulders drop. The thought flashed through my mind that he was giving up, that he was about to take his coat and leave. The hairs on my back prickled in frustration. Surely they could see that this mutual distrust was exactly what the old woman had hoped to achieve, and that if John walked out now, she would have won? I wished I could do something to rescue the situation, to make them realize that they were on the same side. But I knew that, on this occasion, there was nothing I could do but watch.

'Look . . .' When John finally spoke, his voice was conciliatory. 'For what it's worth, I don't believe a word of this letter. Like you said, this woman has clearly had it in for you for a while. But maybe' – Debbie breathed in sharply – 'maybe it is appropriate for me to ask about your past. Not because I'm suspicious of you, but just because I'm interested.'

John sat back in his chair to show that he had said his piece. His words had sounded good to me, but Debbie's face remained stony. Outside, the storm had swept in, blowing sheets of rain horizontally along the parade and rattling the café door in its frame. The sky had darkened to an ominous steel-grey, leaving Debbie and John sitting in near-darkness. I felt my pupils dilate as my eyes adjusted to the low light.

'Well,' she said at last. 'Since you're interested . . .' Her chin dropped and her eyes rested on the table between them as she spoke. 'Sophie's father and I ran a business together in Oxford – property management. He did the hands-on maintenance stuff, and I kept things ticking over in the office at home: answering phone calls, speaking to tenants, that sort of thing. It was my contribution to the household while Sophie was little.' She took a deep, shuddering breath, as if girding herself to continue.

'Andrew decided we should buy a place, rent it out and manage it ourselves. He said managing other people's property was a mug's game, that the real money was made by the landlords. I wasn't sure – property in Oxford's not exactly cheap, and we could only just afford our own mortgage – but he was adamant. He said it would be an investment, a nest egg for our future. He'd already found a place, a repossessed house that was up for auction. The plan was to convert it into flats . . .' Debbie's voice cracked, and her eyes stayed fixed on the table.

John had remained completely motionless while she spoke, listening intently.

'Anyway, we bought it, but the renovations seemed to go on forever. It turned out the property was a wreck: subsidence, damp – you name it. Andrew became obsessed, spending all his time there. Sophie and I hardly ever saw him. Meanwhile I was trying to hold things together at home. The phone was ringing off the hook, tenants complaining that repairs hadn't been done, and landlords saying the rent hadn't been paid. And I told all of them that everything would be okay, that we were on top of it, there was nothing to worry about.' Debbie's face crumpled. 'But there was more to worry about than I realized.' She hung her head, and I could see tears drop into her lap. 'He'd been keeping the rent money,' she said, her voice almost a whisper. 'Taking it from the tenants, but rather than paying the landlords, he'd been pumping it into that money-pit of a house. I only found out when one of the landlords turned up on our doorstep.' Her shoulders shook as she sobbed silently.

'That must have been horrific,' John said.

'That wasn't the worst of it,' Debbie continued. 'When it all came out, the police got involved. Andrew claimed that he knew nothing about it, that I'd been responsible for the company finances and he had no idea what had been going on. We were both charged with obtaining property by deception.'

Debbie had slumped low in her chair. She looked broken, distraught, and I was desperate to comfort her.

'It didn't wash in court, of course,' she went on. 'The bank had evidence that he'd handled all the money transfers. He got nine months, suspended on the basis that it was his first offence. He was liable for court costs and compensation and, because everything was in our joint names, we had to sell our home.' She exhaled a long breath and lifted her chin. 'Of course that was when he decided to tell me that he'd met someone else.'

'The bastard!' John said. Debbie mustered a rueful smile and pulled a tissue out of her pocket to wipe her eyes.

'So there you have it,' she concluded. 'That's my dirty laundry, now aired in public, thanks to a bitter, lonely old woman. Yes, I was once investigated by the police, but my name was cleared. The question is: What are you going to do about it?'

34

Jo and Debbie were in the café kitchen a couple of nights later, preparing for their Friday night takeaway. Jo was reading the letter with a look of growing horror, while Debbie separated the slices of their pizza with a knife.

'The evil witch!' Jo tossed the letter onto the worktop in disgust. 'Please tell me John wasn't taken in by it?'

Debbie shook her head. 'I thought it was touch-and-go for a while, but no, he wasn't taken in. Turns out she used to own this place, and has had it in for anyone who's run it since.'

'It makes my blood boil, Debs – it really does,' Jo replied, prising the lids off two bottles of beer. 'How dare she make accusations like that about you? And in such an underhand way, too. She should at least have the nerve to say it to your face.'

They moved across the café to a table, where Debbie placed the pizza box between them. 'I know and, believe me, I was livid when I first read it. But then I realized that she's just a sad, lonely woman who has nothing better to do with her time than try and ruin other people's lives. She's tried everything else to get at me, and this was her last-ditch attempt.' Debbie took a sip of beer, but Jo's brow remained knitted.

'I think you're being very understanding, Debs. I bet her fingerprints are all over that letter. If it was me, I'd get the police onto her. It's libel!'

Debbie sighed. 'She's not worth it, Jo. She's just a bitter old woman and, despite her best attempts, she's failed. The café's doing better than ever, and John and I are okay. I don't want to waste any more time thinking about her.'

Jo frowned as she took a bite of pizza, seemingly reluctant to let the subject drop. The smell of their meal had drifted up to the flat and the kittens soon appeared at the bottom of the stairs. They sniffed the air hopefully, before running towards the table in search of scraps.

'You know what?' Debbie said, placing a pizza crust on her plate. 'The irony is that if anyone should understand what I've been through, it's her. She went through pretty much the same thing with her husband as I did with Andrew. It's sad, really, when you think about it. She obviously never got over it.'

'Maybe it *is* sad, Debs, but that doesn't give her the right to try and ruin your life. And I don't share your confidence that this was her last-ditch attempt. Who knows what she might try next, if she isn't stopped.'

Debbie shook her head firmly. 'I appreciate your concern, Jo, but really, I wouldn't want to give her the satisfaction of thinking she'd rattled me. It's over – she's lost.'

To make her point, Debbie walked over to the serving counter and picked up the letter, tearing it in half, before dropping it into the bin. When she got back to the table she found that Purdy had jumped into her seat and was sniffing the edge of her plate. Debbie scooped her up and placed her gently but firmly back on the floor.

'Fair enough – it's your call, but I'd keep my wits about me, if I were you.' Jo's eyes were on Purdy, who, having conceded defeat over the pizza, was scampering up the wooden walkway to the hammock. 'And maybe you should keep the kittens indoors for the time being. You wouldn't want them to end up in a stew in the old bat's kitchen.'

Debbie shot a horrified look across the table. 'Jo, how could you even suggest such a thing! She's a bitter old woman, not a psychopath.'

Jo shrugged. 'I hope you're right, Debs. But who knows what she's capable of?'

Debbie chose not to respond, and they carried on eating in silence. When they had finished, Jo placed the cardboard pizza box on the floor and the kittens rushed over, jostling with each other to be the first to get to its contents. I watched as they devoured the drops of melted cheese and clusters of ground beef, oblivious to the conversation going on around them.

I was unable to get Jo's words out of my mind, however. Much as I wanted to believe Debbie, my instincts were telling me that Jo was right – that there was no way of knowing what the old woman might do next. I closed my eyes and pictured the look on her face as she thrust her shopping trolley towards me on the street. She had wanted to hurt me, of that I was certain. She had tried, and failed, to sabotage the café and Debbie's relationship with John. Surely her next step would be to hurt the kittens?

My anxiety did not go away, and in the days that followed I was unable to think about anything else. The kittens would soon be old enough to go outside, and I was terrified to think of what might happen if they encountered the old woman in the street. They had led a blessed life and I was convinced that their trusting, friendly natures would make them an easy target for the battleaxe's ire. It made my blood run cold, just thinking about it.

The summer tourist season in Stourton was under way, the town's population swollen with visitors. Coachloads of tourists were dispatched in the market square on a daily basis, to meander slowly around the town, admiring its picturesque streets and quaint stone cottages. They wandered in and out of shops in pairs or small clusters, filling their shopping bags with souvenirs and edible treats. As they passed along the cobbled parade they would often pause outside the café window, pointing at me through the glass. When they pushed the door open, their faces lit up with delight as the kittens rushed over to greet them.

The customers were happy, the kittens relished all the attention, and Debbie was thrilled with the café's popularity, but still I could not relax. I felt like I was standing guard over my kittens, convinced that – if I dropped my guard – the old lady would pounce. Adrenaline surged through my body every time I heard the rattle of her trolley outside the window. I stared defiantly at her through the glass, but she never once looked at me, keeping her lips pursed and her eyes on the street ahead.

About a week after Jo and Debbie's conversation, I heard Debbie talking on the phone, booking an appointment with the vet to have the kittens microchipped. I knew that meant they would soon be free to roam outside, and that I would be unable to protect them from the old woman any longer. I had no choice but to act; if I did nothing, I felt sure I would never have peace of mind again.

When the café opened that morning, I jumped onto the window cushion and waited. As soon as the old woman appeared on the other side of the street, I slipped out of the café and followed her.

She walked briskly to the end of the parade, where she turned right and headed towards the market square. I trotted behind her at a discreet distance, dodging a friendly tourist who tried to stroke me. When she reached the square, the old woman went into the fish-monger's and I darted under a parked car to catch my breath. I hadn't visited the square since I had first arrived in Stourton as a homeless stray, and I was over-whelmed by the noise and activity that assaulted me from all sides.

It was difficult to reconcile the hectic scene around me with the lonely square I had encountered at Christmas. It was market day, and packs of tourists surged along the pavements, spilling off the kerbs into the path of passing traffic. Shoppers moved slowly between the market stalls, gimlet-eyed as they searched for bargains, tugging dogs or bored children after them. The lively, bustling atmosphere could not be more different from the ambience I had experienced on my first night, but, in my agitated state, it felt no less daunting.

The old woman stepped out of the fishmonger's and made her way across to the far side of the square. I dashed out from under the car and ran over the road, glimpsing the wheels of her trolley as they disappeared into a crowd of shoppers. I pushed into the melee, weaving between legs and pushchairs, and reached the pavement just in time to see her turn down an alley between two shops. I padded closer, peering gingerly around the alley's entrance. Up ahead, the woman was rapidly disappearing down the passageway and I knew I had to follow. I took a deep breath and entered the alley, automatically dropping to a defensive prowl.

The sounds of the market dropped away, and the rattle of the trolley's wheels filled the enclosed path, magnified by the stone walls on both sides. I felt a prickling sensation on the back of my neck, the primitive instinct that warned me that I was being watched. Panicked, I glanced up to see a pair of cat's eyes staring intently from the top of the wall beside me. My hackles rose in expectation of an attack, but the cat remained motionless, its eyes fixed with an expression that seemed curious rather than hostile.

A succession of confused images flashed through my mind, memories that had lain dormant for many months. I knew that I recognized the cat, but it took a few seconds to realize that it was the tortoiseshell I had found sleeping on a shed roof, soon after my arrival in Stourton. This was her alley; the same one I had wandered into the morning after my attack by the ginger tomcat. I felt a rush of gratitude when I saw her; it was thanks to her advice that I had sought out the churchyard for shelter, and consequently discovered the alleyway behind the café. I thought I detected a glimmer of recognition in her eye and I blinked at her, wishing I had time to thank her, belatedly, for what she had done for me. But I knew that, if I lingered, I would lose sight of the old woman, so I ran on, feeling the tortoiseshell's inquisitive gaze still on my back.

At the end of the alley, the woman turned into a terrace of neat brick houses. She crossed the road and walked towards the last house in the row, standing her trolley on the pavement while she opened the garden gate. I darted under the hedge that bordered the front of the garden, and raced towards her front door. While she was fastening the gate shut behind her, I lay down on the path in front of her doorstep and closed my eyes.

I felt the path beneath me vibrate as her trolley rolled towards me. Inches from my prostrate body, the trolley stopped, and I half-opened one eye. The old woman surveyed me with a look of disgust. 'Scram, cat.

Clear off!' she said, nudging my leg with the tip of her shoe. I remained motionless and let out a pained yowl. Shocked, she leaned forwards, using her shopping trolley for support as she bent down to examine me more closely. She prodded me lightly on the flank with her finger and I let out another cry of pain, at which she straightened up, tutting in consternation.

I saw her cast a furtive look over her shoulder, as if checking to see that she was alone. She took her trolley tightly by the handle, and my heart began to thump in my chest. When I had set off in pursuit of her I had a hazy notion that, by confronting her, I would call her bluff. Now it had started to dawn on me that, in fact, she was about to call mine. Rather than putting an end to her campaign of harassment against Debbie, I had presented her with the perfect opportunity to finish what she had started: to run me over with her trolley and dispose of me in the privacy of her own home.

She yanked the trolley forward, but suddenly veered onto the grass, skirting around me as if I were roadkill. I felt a surge of relief that I was unharmed, which quickly turned to disappointment. Was she simply going to ignore me, leaving me – dying, for all she knew – in her front garden? I lay on the path, holding my breath, willing her not to go inside. I sensed she was looking at me, and I imagined her face, lips pursed, eyes narrowed as she considered her options. I was sure she was convinced I was gravely injured. Would it occur to her that, if I was found dead outside her house, she would be the prime suspect?

I heard slow footsteps on the path behind me. 'What's wrong with you?' Her voice was irritable and impatient. Keeping my eyes tightly shut, I began to whimper pitifully. 'Oh, for goodness' sake,' she tutted.

My ears twitched at the sound of the shopping trolley being unzipped behind me, followed by rustling noises as she moved its contents around. I felt one hand slide underneath my hind legs and another under my shoulders, but I lay still, fighting the natural urge to jump out of her hands and run away. She lifted my limp body off the path and I could hear her shallow breathing as she lowered me carefully into the trolley.

I opened my eyes in time to see her face disappear as she slid the zip shut above me.

35

It was stiflingly close inside the trolley, and pitch black, but for a chink of daylight through a gap in the zip. The sharp corner of a piece of packaging dug into my flesh, and I twisted onto all fours to absorb the impact as the trolley's wheels bounced along the ground beneath me. There was a strong stench of mackerel emanating from the plastic bag under my paws which, combined with the airlessness and rocking motion of the trolley, made me feel nauseous. I slowed my breathing in an effort to fight the growing queasiness in my belly: I didn't know what the old lady had planned for me, but I suspected that vomiting over her shopping would not help my cause.

Desperate for fresh air, I began to tug at the zip above me until it snagged on my claw and I was able to work it slowly back along its track. As soon as the gap was large enough, I poked my head through and saw the lady's knuckles gripping the trolley handle just a few inches from my nose. My relief at breathing fresh air was short-lived, however, as I scanned my surroundings, wondering where she was taking me. There were walls on both sides, and the woman's back blocked my view ahead.

I stood up on my hind legs and extended my neck as far as I could, trying to see around her body. Something moved at the edge of my vision and I twisted my head, to see the tortoiseshell cat staring back at me. The quizzical semi-recognition I had seen in her eyes on my first journey through the alley had been replaced by a look of bafflement. I blinked at her for the second time that morning, well aware of how bizarre I must look, with my disembodied head protruding from an old woman's trolley. The tortoiseshell's tail twitched and she watched in amused silence as I was wheeled past.

As we neared the end of the alley I dropped back down beneath the zip, not wanting to draw attention to myself from passers-by. I could hear the noise of the market square around me, the slam of car doors and the shuffle of feet on the pavement, and before long I felt the uneven bump of cobbles underneath the trolley's wheels. We stopped, then I heard a bell tinkle as a door opened, followed by a lurching sensation as the trolley was pulled inside.

Relief washed over me as I recognized the familiar sounds of the café around me: the hum of conversation and clink of teacups, and scratching sounds as one of the kittens went to work on a nearby scratching post.

'Excuse me,' I heard the old woman say.

A moment's silence, then Debbie's voice, sounding surprised, 'Oh. Can I help you?'

I could imagine Debbie's shocked expression upon finding herself face-to-face with the woman who had done so much to hurt her.

'I've got your cat,' the woman mumbled.

'I'm sorry?' Debbie answered, and there was no mistaking the fear in her voice. I knew she would be thinking of her conversation with Jo, regretting that she hadn't paid more heed to her friend's warnings that the battle axe couldn't be trusted.

'She was on my doorstep, I think she might be injured,' the old lady stammered.

When Debbie answered, she sounded angry and suspicious, 'Molly? Are you sure? Well, where is she?'

Before she could answer, I popped my head through the gap in the zip. Debbie gasped and watched, speechless, as I wriggled out of the trolley and jumped onto the floor.

'Molly!' exclaimed Debbie, rushing towards me. I stood up to greet her, aware of the dumbfounded expression on the old woman's face.

'I – er . . . she was yowling. I thought she was hurt,' she explained, bewildered by the sight of me in evident good health. I felt a glimmer of pity for the old lady. Although she was telling the truth, her faltering delivery made her sound guilty and unconvincing.

Debbie ignored her, however, as she knelt on the floor to check me all over. Reassured that I was unharmed, she turned to face the old woman. 'Well, she seems to be all right now.'

'I – er . . . I thought . . .' The old woman was beginning to blush, aware that Debbie was scrutinizing her distrustfully. 'Well, if she's okay, I suppose I'll be getting on.' She began to fiddle with the zip on her trolley, unable to bear Debbie's gaze any longer.

Debbie watched as the old lady busied herself with her trolley, her face turning a shade of red that almost matched the colour of her hair. I sensed that Debbie was beginning to feel sorry for the woman, whose mortification and discomfort were plain to see. 'Can I get you anything?' she offered, politely. The old lady looked startled and, although she opened her mouth to reply, no sound came out. 'A cup of tea, perhaps?' Debbie suggested.

The woman closed her mouth and glanced down at her feet. 'I don't think . . . I'm not . . .'

Debbie smiled, aware that her friendliness had

caught the old woman off-guard, and allowing her time to reply.

'Well, I suppose, since I'm here, a cup of tea wouldn't hurt,' the old woman said at last, casting a nervous look at Debbie, who smiled and grabbed a menu, before leading the woman across the café to a table near the fireplace.

As soon as she had sat down, the old lady was surrounded by the kittens, who were drawn across the café by the smell of mackerel drifting from her shopping trolley. They crawled underneath it and sniffed her shoes and skirt, while I loitered nearby, watching her reactions closely. At first she seemed alarmed by the kittens' inquisitiveness, nervously trying to move her bag and trolley away from them as they scampered around her, but after a few moments she seemed to relax, accepting that their curiosity was playful rather than menacing.

Debbie brought a pot of tea across the café, and placed a Feline Fancy next to it on the table. The woman stared at the cake, which was decorated with a pink nose and whiskers, then looked up at Debbie in confusion. 'It's on the house,' Debbie explained. 'Thank you for bringing Molly home.'

The old lady's face softened. 'That's very kind,' she replied quietly, smiling at the cake. I padded towards her and, as she took her first sip of tea, pressed my body

gently into the side of her leg. Instinctively, and without saying a word, she lowered her hand to stroke my
back.

'I can't believe you gave her a Feline Fancy, Mum.'
Sophie sounded affronted by her mother's willingness
to forgive the old woman's transgressions. John had
come over and the three of them were eating dinner
at the dining table. Sophie dropped her cutlery, to
emphasize her indignation. 'After everything she's done
to us! Did she even say sorry for any of it?'

Debbie sighed. 'Well, she didn't apologize as such,
but we had a chat before she left, and she was very
complimentary about the café. I got the feeling she
really is sorry.' She smiled hopefully at Sophie, whose
face remained defiantly sceptical. 'And besides,' Debbie
went on, 'I think the old dear must have a screw loose
somewhere – why else would she zip a perfectly healthy
cat inside her shopping trolley and invent some story
about her being half-dead?'

I was having a wash on the sofa, but I smiled
inwardly, congratulating myself on my acting skills.

John had remained silent throughout Debbie's
account of the day's drama but, at this, he started to
chuckle softly.

'What's so funny?' Debbie asked, sensing mockery
in the air.

'Nothing,' he replied with a placatory smile. Now it was Debbie's turn to put her cutlery down as she looked at John to explain. He took the hint. 'It's just that . . . has it occurred to you that she might have been telling the truth? That she really did find Molly lying in her garden, playing dead?'

'*Playing dead?*' Debbie snorted derisively. 'I hardly think so, John. Why would Molly do that? You can see for yourself that she's as fit as a fiddle.'

All three of them looked at me, but I carried on with my wash, feigning ignorance.

'Well,' John said, spreading his palms upwards in a 'who knows' gesture, 'maybe it is just a coincidence. The old woman happened to find Molly in her garden, thought she was injured when in fact she wasn't, and decided to bring her back to the café. It could be that simple. But I think you're underestimating that cat, Debbie. I think she knows more than she's letting on.'

I flicked a glance towards the table, and caught sight of John smiling at me. Blushing, I turned away and busied myself with grooming the base of my spine. John was right of course; I knew much more than I was letting on, and not just about what had happened that day with the battleaxe.

I knew how many challenges Debbie had faced since taking me in, both personally and professionally. I knew how she had been pushed to breaking point by the demands of a failing business and a struggling teenager, and yet still found room, in her home and her heart, for a stray cat and a litter of kittens. I knew there was a time when it had seemed that we might cost her her livelihood, yet she never once sought to blame us. She had held onto us when our very existence must have been a burden, and I had repaid her the only way I could: by comforting her when she was in despair, and by using every power at my disposal to make sure she found the happiness she deserved. Whether she underestimated what I had done for her was irrelevant. She was my owner, after all, and taking care of her was my job.

Epilogue

It is Christmas morning. A full year has passed since my arrival in Stourton, and I am on the dining table watching Sophie and Debbie unwrap their presents on the living-room floor. There is a small stocking of cat treats under the tree, a gift to us all from Margery, but the kittens are more interested in shredding the discarded wrapping paper strewn across the floor. They are lithe young cats now; their limbs are long and muscular and their fluffy fur has been replaced by sleek pelts. But the excitement of Christmas has brought out their playful exuberance, reminding me fondly of their younger selves.

Debbie gets up to go into the kitchen, and Sophie leans against the sofa, engrossed in her new mobile phone, a gift from her mother. Sophie isn't looking at me, but I blink at her anyway. I am fond of Sophie, and I know she is of me. She no longer exudes pent-up anger whenever I am around, and I can't remember the last time she called me a fleabag, or complained about my hair on her clothes. Sometimes I even sleep on her bed.

Downstairs, the bell above the café door tinkles.

'That you, John?' Debbie calls, over the noise of the kitchen radio.

'No, it's Father Christmas,' John replies.

'Even better!' Debbie laughs. 'Come on up. I hope you've remembered the orange juice – I could murder a Buck's Fizz right now!'

There is a pause. 'You might just want to come down here first,' John says.

Debbie steps into the hallway, perplexed. 'Why – what is it? Please don't tell me it's the boiler again . . .'

'No, it's not the boiler. It's just that there's someone here who seems to want to come in.'

Alarm flickers across Debbie's face. She takes off her apron and heads downstairs to the café. Intrigued, I jump off the dining table and follow her.

John is standing by the door in the empty café, loosening the scarf around his neck. I register the bag of wrapped gifts on the floor by his feet, and I am aware that he steps towards Debbie and kisses her. 'Happy Christmas,' I hear him say.

But I am not looking at them. I am looking at the window.

Perched precariously on the windowsill outside is a cat. He is looking over his shoulder at the street behind, his ears flicking in the wind. He looks nervous, twitchy, as if he is fighting the urge to run.

Sophie has come downstairs too, followed by the kittens, who want to know where everyone has gone. Now we are all standing in the café, looking at the cat on the windowsill. The cat turns back to face the café and his eye catches mine through the glass.

'That cat looks just like Eddie!' Sophie exclaims.

'Indeed he does,' Debbie agrees. I am not looking at her, but I know she is watching me, and I can hear the smile in her voice. I feel like I am frozen to the spot, dumbfounded.

'Someone must have told him Molly's Cat Café is the place to be,' John jokes. 'He's a handsome chap, too. You've got room for another one, haven't you, Debs?'

Debbie pauses, and I can feel her eyes on me. 'What do you think, Molly, shall I let him in?'

Hearing her say my name rouses me from my daze. I turn and look at her, but my mind is blank. She laughs at me, but her laugh is not unkind. It's a laugh that suggests she knows what's going on, and that she understands. I watch as she opens the café door and leans out.

'Come on, puss, in you come,' she calls.

The tomcat looks at her and I see his tail twitch. I remember his words to me in the alley: *I'm not really a 'nice lady' kind of cat.* Surely this café full of strangers will be too daunting for his solitary nature? His tail twitches again and his green eyes turn back to me. It occurs to me that he is waiting for me to invite him in. I blink at him slowly, and immediately he jumps down onto the pavement. A moment later he is standing inside the doorway, his head held high in a show of confidence that must have taken more courage than he is letting on. The kittens rush over to him, fascinated and slightly in awe of this mysterious stranger.

'Well, I guess that's settled,' Debbie laughs. 'I suppose I'd better set another place at the table!'

I creep forward. My mind is buzzing with questions, but the kittens are crowding around the tomcat, all eager to be first in line for his attention. He patiently allows them to sniff him, but then his eyes look up to find mine and I can see they are smiling.

It is mid-afternoon, and the tomcat and I have left everyone eating turkey in the café, to head out into the empty streets of Stourton. We pad along the alleyway behind the café, down through the churchyard, and start to wander towards the square, our only witnesses the cawing crows on the chimney stacks. There is a chill in the air and, as the tomcat and I walk, we stick close to each other's side, our footsteps naturally falling into a shared rhythm.

'So, where have you been all this time?' I ask, shyly. Glancing at the side of his face, I notice he's gained a few scars since I last saw him.

'Oh, just wandering,' the tomcat replies, wrinkling his nose. 'Life on the road isn't all it's cracked up to be,' he says sagely.

'I could have told you that,' I joke.

'And besides,' he adds, 'I missed the tuna mayonnaise.'

I stop walking, momentarily affronted, but then he catches my eye and I realize he is teasing me.

We turn the corner into the market square. The winter daylight is beginning to fade, low clouds scud across the sky and, above them, the pale crescent moon is already visible. All around us the square is decked out for Christmas. Colourful lights blink prettily in every window, and the tree in the middle of the square points vigorously upward, wreathed in white bulbs. Devoid of people and traffic, the square feels like it belongs to us, and us alone.

I wonder how it is possible for Stourton to look just as it did a year ago, as if nothing has changed. So much has changed for me in the last twelve months that I sometimes feel like a different cat from the one who arrived, rain-soaked and half-starved, after weeks in the open country. I feel sorry for the cat I was then, so desperate for someone to take pity on me and give me a home. And yet I am also proud of that cat. Pitiful she may have been, but were it not for her determination, I would not be here now.

The tomcat and I have made our way back to the cobbled street outside the café. The blinds are drawn, but I can see slivers of light around the edges of the window, and hear Debbie singing along to Christmas music inside. The tomcat is standing to one side on the doorstep, allowing me, chivalrously, to enter the café first. I nudge the door open and the warm atmosphere inside the café envelops us.

At a glance, I take in the crackling fire in the stove, our kittens dozing around the room, and the smiling faces of Debbie, Sophie and John as they read aloud jokes from their Christmas crackers. The tomcat stands beside me, gazing benignly at the scene before us, and I swell with pride to think of how much the café has changed since it became my home. But I also feel humble, because I know that the journey I have been on over the past year was not just about finding a home; it was about finding myself. I have been many different cats since losing Margery: a desperate stray, a self-sufficient alley-cat, a cherished pet, and a loving mother. I have been all of those cats, and they will always remain a part of me, because they have made me who I am.

The Real Cat Cafés

I first became aware of the existence of cat cafés in 2014. As a cat fanatic, I loved the idea of relaxing in a café full of laid-back felines. But I was also intrigued to imagine how a cat café comes into being, and what the background stories of the cats in such a place might be.

This was how the idea for *Molly and the Cat Café* was born. Although its inspiration comes from the real cat cafés, however, it is a work of fiction. When writing about Molly's cat café, I sometimes had to allow the demands of plot and character to take precedence over factual accuracy. So it seems only fair to correct some misconceptions the book may have conveyed about the work done by the real cat cafés.

Japan is considered to be the spiritual home of the cat café: there are said to be nearly forty in Tokyo alone. In recent years, cat cafés have begun to appear around the world, springing up in Asia, North America, Australia and across Europe. In Britain there are currently cat cafés in London, Edinburgh, Newcastle, Nottingham and Birmingham, with more planned for other parts of the country.

In addition to providing cat-loving humans with access to feline company, the cat cafés often have another purpose: to find permanent homes for their residents. Whereas Molly and her kittens are Debbie's pets, many of the real cat cafés source their cats from local rescue shelters, and offer up the cats in their care for adoption.

The cats' welfare is of the utmost importance for the cat cafés. Great care is taken to build a colony, usually of around a dozen cats, who will live peacefully alongside each other and whose temperaments suit the sociable atmosphere of a café. Precautions are taken to limit the number of customers allowed in the café at any one time in order to prevent the cats becoming stressed, and advance bookings are often necessary. Although some cat cafés provide outside space for their cats, others keep their cats indoors. I imagine the cats are unlikely to come and go as they please in the way that Molly does from her café.

Molly and the Cat Café is not intended to be a factually accurate account of a real cat café; it is the story of one cat and her search for a home. It is about the bond that forms between us and our feline companions; the strength of our love for them and, I would like to think, of their love for us. I believe it is the universal nature of this bond that drives the phenomenon of the cat café to worldwide success.

MD, *June 2015*

This book would not exist were it not for the help and support of many people. Thanks to my editor Victoria Hughes-Williams and all the team at Pan Macmillan for your enthusiasm and input at every stage of this process; to my agents Diane and Kate at Diane Banks Associates for your commitment and professionalism; and to Claire Morrison at Maison de Moggy in Edinburgh, for taking the time to tell me how a real cat café works.

Special thanks also to Debbie, for allowing me to base my (human) heroine on you.

Big gratitude and love to Suse and Louis for your patience, and to Phil for carrying more than your fair share of the domestic burden so that I could write. I couldn't have done it without you.